PAIGE DEVEREAUX

BERNADETTE MARIE

5 PRINCE PUBLISHING

Published by 5 PRINCE PUBLISHING & BOOKS, LLC

PO Box 865, Arvada, CO 80001

www.5PrinceBooks.com

Digital ISBN: 978-1-63112-258-3

Print ISBN: 978-1-63112-259-0

Cover Credit: Marianne Nowicki

To Stan,
Thank you for always having my back.
I love you.
Forever and a day!

ACKNOWLEDGMENTS

Tony, Nick, Garrett, Stanley, and Jack, I love writing these stories with brothers and friends. It's a lovely thing to be able to bring such amazing relationships to life because I am surrounded by them.

Mom and Sissy I miss pink stores, yoga studios, and tap houses. I can't wait to enjoy these things with you again.

Cate, may these stories continue to heal us and amuse us. Thank you for taking this journey with me. I appreciate you so much!

To my hive, Thank you all for racing through these and making them even more amazing.

To my readers, I can't thank you enough for coming back time after time.

OTHER TITLES BY

BERNADETTE MARIE

THE KELLER FAMILY SERIES

The Executive's Decision

A Second Chance

Opposite Attraction

Center Stage

Lost and Found

Love Songs

Home Run

The Acceptance

The Merger

The Escape Clause

A Romance for Christmas

THE WALKER FAMILY SERIES

Walker Pride

Stargazing

Walker Bride

Wanderlust

Walker Revenge

Victory

Walker Spirit

Beginnings

Walker Defense

Masterpiece

At Last

THE MATCHMAKER SERIES

Matchmakers

Encore

Finding Hope

THE THREE MRS. MONROES TRILOGY

Amelia

Penelope

Vivian

THE ASPEN CREEK SERIES

First Kiss

Unexpected Admirer

On Thin Ice

Indomitable Spirit

THE DENVER BRIDE SERIES

Cart Before the Horse

Never Saw it Coming

Candy Kisses

ROMANTIC SUSPENSE

Chasing Shadows

PARANORMAL ROMANCES

The Tea Shop

The Last Goodbye

HOLIDAY FAVORITES

Corporate Christmas

Tropical Christmas

THE DEVEREAUX FAMILY SERIES

Kennedy Devereaux

Chase Devereaux

Max Devereaux

Paige Devereaux

PAIGE DEVEREAUX

CHAPTER 1

With her finger on the mouse, Paige scrolled through the website, taking in the sights and reading up on Oahu. As she looked at the tropical scenes splayed across her computer screen, she was making a mental list as to what to pack, how to do her hair, and where the best beaches were to do yoga in the mornings.

Paige's father had met a woman nearly a year ago on a cruise ship, and now they were getting married. And wasn't his timing perfect? In the past year, her sister and both of her brothers had gotten married too. She, on the other hand, was apparently destined to be a bridesmaid for the rest of her life.

Sitting back on the exercise ball she used for a desk chair, she picked up her cup of tea and sipped. The mint flavor invigorated her tongue and her nose.

She didn't usually think too much of marriage, but she'd been inundated with it lately, that was for sure. Things had changed quickly, but when it came to Paige's life, that was normal.

Paige was only seven when her mother was killed in a car accident, and soon Kennedy and Chase were living with her and their father. But, already teenagers by that time, it wasn't long before they moved out and headed off to college and then onto new things in their lives. Eventually Paige got old enough to do the college thing and then the job thing.

Still only in her late twenties, Paige was motivated by her older siblings and their ambitious career choices. Her sister Kennedy owned a stylish boutique, where Paige worked once in a while. Kennedy had married Joel, who owned a tap house with his brother and business partners—and Paige filled in there once in a while too. Chase, her oldest brother, owned a limousine service, and Max, the next oldest, had recently sold his booming construction business to marry the woman of his dreams. Now he was remodeling his wife's childhood home for them to live in.

Entrepreneurship was in her blood. For the past year, Paige had been working and saving to purchase the wellness center where she taught yoga. Her vision was to expand the yoga studio and bring in massage therapists. The woman who currently owned the wellness center was waiting for Paige to make her offer, but she knew time was slipping away. If she didn't come up with the money soon, the current owner just might offer the business to someone else.

Paige could borrow the money from her siblings, but there was some pride in doing it all herself—no loans. Though each of her siblings, and their spouses, had offered to carry her.

As Paige clicked to the next tropical photo, she let the mixture of her emotions stir in her chest. There was nothing she wanted more than a nice vacation in Hawaii in November. And she was thrilled for her father, who had finally found a woman that he loved enough he wanted to get married again. On the other hand, was the man crazy for planning a destination wedding?

A destination wedding in November wasn't helping anyone. She knew the scheduling challenges it was bringing to her siblings. Kennedy and Joel had to adjust their businesses and think of taking a one-year-old to Hawaii. Chase and his wife Hillary were in exactly the same boat with his business and their daughter. Max and his wife Meghann were settling into newlywed life. They didn't have children yet, but Meghann had just been offered a new contract to promote some pasta brand, which included a new cooking show. This time, however, Meghann was calling the shots, so maybe Hawaii wasn't as daunting a thought or task as it was to the rest of them.

For Paige, it meant paying for a trip and days without work. That certainly wasn't helping her bankroll.

She sipped her tea and when her cell phone rang, she glanced at the screen before making a move to pick it up. The face of Oliver, one of her brother-in-law's business partners at the tap house, popped up on the screen and made her laugh. They'd gone for a hike together once, and he'd worn the silliest of hats. She'd snapped the photo when he wasn't looking and set it for his contact photo. Whenever he called, she got a good laugh out of it.

Paige picked up the phone and swiped her finger over the screen.

"Hey, Oliver. What's up?"

"How'd you know it was me?"

She laughed. "Seriously?" Sometimes she didn't know if he was serious or not. The noises from his end of the call told her he was at the tap house. No doubt on a Saturday night they were busier than the rest of the week.

"Tell me you're not busy right now, or out on a date, or already in bed."

"It's seven o'clock. I'm not in bed."

"On a date?"

"Almost never on a date."

She heard a man place his order and a woman laugh in the background.

Oliver cleared his throat. "What do you think about coming down here and helping out? Joel, Jeff, and Craig are all here," he said, naming his business partners. "We are fully staffed, but we are still slammed. Kennedy is coming down to help too. Hillary is going to watch the baby. Chase has too many fares, so he's out driving. But we could really use a hand."

Paige stood from her exercise ball and started for her bedroom. "What's going on? Why are you so busy?"

"We overbooked food trucks, so we have three of them here. They're super popular on social media and they drew a crowd. There was some college football game up the road too, and—" he stopped talking to her and had an exchange with someone else before coming back to their conversation. "Anyway, what do you say? Can you come help out?"

Paige wasn't one to turn down work, especially if it was that busy. Tips would be plentiful. "I'll be there in twenty."

"You're the best, Paige. Love ya!" he shouted as he disconnected the call.

Paige looked down at the blank screen. *Love ya!* The words still resonated in her ear, but humored her all the same. He was a good pal, that's all there was to it.

CHAPTER 2

Kennedy carried a tray of glasses behind the bar and Oliver quickly moved out of her way.

"One of these days, I'm going to cost us an entire tray of glass," Oliver joked as he moved to the shelf and pulled down two more glasses.

"Well, do it someday when I'm not carrying them," Kennedy joked as she set the tray on the counter and blew a wayward piece of hair from her face. "I need fifteen minutes in the office—alone," she said with a stressed grin.

"Okay," Oliver drew out the word, and then realized she was in need of time to use her breast pump. He was grateful that she hadn't actually said it aloud, he might have dropped the glasses in his hand.

"I'll be back shortly."

Oliver watched as Kennedy hurried away and her husband Joel skirted the bar. "She'll be back in..."

"Ya, she told me," Oliver interrupted Joel before he finished the sentence. "Paige is on her way down. She said she could help out."

"We really should think about getting some more glasses for

nights like these. Luckily it's still nice outside with the heaters on the patio, or we'd be at max capacity."

Oliver put one of the glasses under the tap and pulled the handle. "I'm just going to say we're lucky right? If we get ticketed for being at capacity, it's okay?"

"It's not okay, but yeah, we're lucky," Joel agreed as he filled two glasses from the tap. "Did you eat yet tonight?"

"Not yet."

Joel nodded as he walked toward the other end of the bar. "I'll have them put in a pizza for us."

"Veggie," Oliver reminded him, or he knew he'd get a pizza filled with processed meats.

"How are we even friends?" Joel laughed as he slipped out from behind the bar.

Oliver filled a flight for a table of women who had wandered in and asked for shots. It never failed. Not everyone understood a tap room. They didn't carry hard liquor, and he wasn't sure he could handle women who wanted to drink shots all night. They poured the finest craft beers from local breweries and had food trucks lined up every night of the week for different tastes. It was a fine way to make a living, he thought as he watched Kennedy emerge from the office. Not only did he get to spend his days, and nights, with the men he considered to be his brothers in spirit, but their families were involved too.

Oliver thought of his parents and his grandparents as he filled another order. Half of his childhood had been spent in a teepee. His hair had hung well past his shoulders, and he was seven when he got a pair of sneakers. That had been a fine birthday.

As a teenager he'd always wonder if the stories his grandparents told him were true, how they'd taken him to live with them when he was eight because they were lonely. But as an adult he knew the real reason. Living with his parents in a *free* community wasn't safe. The image of his mother flashed in his mind from the last time he'd seen her, and he knew his grandparents had saved his life.

Oliver watched Paige walk through the back door, hanging her coat on the peg and grabbing an apron from the shelf.

She was tying the apron around her waist when she slipped in behind him at the bar.

"I don't think I've ever seen this place this busy," she laughed as she positioned herself next to Oliver. "Seriously, if you're this packed this weekend, what do you think Halloween is going to look like next week?"

"I don't even want to think about it," Oliver admitted as he closed out another order. "You'll be here, right?"

"All hands on deck. I'm in."

"Thank goodness Joel married into a big family."

Paige laughed and it brought out the pink in her cheeks Oliver noticed as he pulled from another tap.

Kennedy brought back another tray of empty glasses. "Hey, Joel called you too, huh?"

Paige shook her head. "Nah, this guy needed a sidekick." She nodded in Oliver's direction. "He pulled me away from the computer where I was studying the layout of Oahu."

Kennedy shook her head. "I don't know what he's thinking. Actually, he's not thinking," she referred to their father. "Two one-year-olds on a plane for hours? The very thought of it gives me anxiety."

Oliver agreed that just hearing it was giving him anxiety. As he pulled the next beer, he blew out a breath. "Have to change out the keg. I'll be right back," he said dismissing himself to the back room behind the bar where the kegs ran to the taps.

He swapped out one keg for another. It had been one of the most popular beers they had on tap, and it had been his call to bring it in.

Oliver chuckled to himself. He knew he didn't have it in him to actually follow through with brewing. Besides, luck was never on his side, and he was surprised that his partners hadn't caught on to that yet. If he were to brew his own beer, he'd probably blow up the building. That was the kind of luck Westcotts had.

Rolling the empty keg out and stacking it with the other empties, he walked back out to the bar.

"All set," he said as Paige handed him a glass.

"That one is pretty popular."

"Have you tried it?" he asked.

"Not yet."

Oliver pulled down a small taster glass and filled it. He handed it to Paige and watched as she sipped it.

The expression on her face said she was dissecting it with her taste buds. "That's crisp. Watermelon?" she asked and Oliver nodded.

"Do you like it?"

"I really do. Maybe I'll have one later."

"We'll have one together," he promised. "When this madness dies down."

CHAPTER 3

The food trucks had packed up and driven away. Patrons had finished their drinks and the crowd had thinned out long before closing.

Joel and Kennedy had left before ten o'clock, and at midnight Jeff went home to his family. Craig continued to put chairs on tables and sweep the floors, and Paige diligently washed glasses until they were all clean and stacked on the shelves behind the bar.

Oliver wiped down the bar and let out a breath. "There's something about closing up. You know, tidying up, and turning off the lights."

Paige let out a laugh. "I'll remember that since you're the usually the last one to roll up your mat and leave yoga class."

Oliver raised his brow and puckered his lips. "Now that I know you have to tidy up before turning out the lights, I'll stay longer and help."

Paige laughed again. "Okay, I'll hold you to that. I guess I'll head out."

"I thought we were having a beer," Oliver reminded her as he pulled down two glasses.

"It's two o'clock in the morning."

"And?"

"And I guess we're having a beer."

Craig emerged from the back room, his jacket in his hand. "Are you two hanging here?"

Oliver held up a glass. "We're sampling that watermelon one. Interested?"

"Not in the least," Craig pulled on his jacket. "I can't think of anything that sounds worse at two in the morning. I'll see you two later." He gave them a small wave and let himself out the back door.

Oliver filled the glasses from the tap and handed her one. Paige examined it.

"I'm not sure it comes with rave reviews after what Craig said."

"Yeah, but he has no taste," Oliver informed her before he took a long sip.

Paige lifted the glass to her lips and tasted the beer that Oliver enjoyed. She let it sit on her tongue a moment before swallowing. Then she took another sip.

"Well?"

She looked at him and nodded. "I like it."

"You have taste."

Oliver walked around to the other side of the bar and took a seat at one of the stools.

Paige watched him relax with his arms on the bar. She thought maybe they were drinking down their beer and going home, but Oliver looked as if he were settling in. Was she supposed to sit with him?

She sipped her beer and studied the man across from her, whom over the past year and a half had become a good friend.

Oliver was easygoing, and easy on the eyes too, though not Paige's type, and that was some of his charm. Sipping on her watermelon beer, she saw him differently. His hair was shaved on the sides, but with enough length on top to give it some style, when enough product was added. Or, as she had seen it after a hike or yoga class, that boyish flop that would brush across his forehead. Unlike his business partners who wore beards that were either a few days growth or overgrown completely, Oliver's was meticulously groomed at all times. Why at that moment did she want to touch it?

Instead, she drank her beer.

Oliver sat across from her looking down into his glass. Surely he was tired after having been at work all day. She wondered if he was expected to open the next morning too.

"You doing okay?" she asked, finishing her drink.

Oliver lifted his eyes to meet hers. "Yeah, I just get deep in thought at this time of night."

Paige decided to walk around the bar and sit on the stool next to him. "What's on your mind, pal?"

He chuckled at that. "I got a letter from my mom the other day."

"A letter?"

"You've heard of them? Someone writes it by hand, puts it in an envelope..."

"Stamps and all? Yeah, I've heard of them. I just didn't know people did that kind of thing anymore."

"I guess they do." He lifted his glass to his lips and sipped his beer. Then he held the glass in front of him and studied the logo on it before setting it back down. "Haven't heard from her in over twenty years."

"Really?"

"This gets deep fast, doesn't it? We should lock up and go home. I have to be back here in like ten hours."

Paige reached out and placed her hand on his arm, noticing the tattoo she covered as she did so. "Every family is unique. I know what I'm talking about there," she humored, and he smiled. "If you ever want to talk..."

"Thanks. It's not a favorite subject of mine. I'm actually surprised I said that much."

"Then I'm honored that you did that in my presence."

Oliver ran his hand over his beard before drinking down what was left in his glass. He let out a breath when he'd finished, and then picked up both of their glasses, carried them to the sink and set them inside.

"I appreciate you, Paige," he said turning to look at her. "I appreciate all of you. Joel married into a good family, and in turn you've all become part of my family."

"I guess we all have become that, haven't we?"

"The fact that at any moment my partners or I can call a Devereaux, or a spouse, and they show up to help, that says a lot."

She supposed it did. Paige and her siblings were tight, regardless of the fact that they'd been brought up in three different homes. They owed that to their father, no matter how messed up his situations were back then.

Paige hopped off her bar stool, gave her neck a stretch, and pulled off the apron that was still tied around her waist.

"If you need any help tomorrow," she paused and rethought what she'd said. "If you need any help later today, let me know."

Oliver turned off the lights near the bar, then walked to the front doors and made sure they were locked. "No yoga classes?"

"My Sunday classes weren't widely attended, so I cancelled them for now."

"And you're still looking to buy the wellness center?"

Paige nodded. "I need a little more money. I can't make the offer yet."

"Did you apply for a loan?"

"I don't want a loan. I can't see paying someone else for me to be in business."

They walked toward the back room and Paige tossed her apron in the laundry bin by the door before picking up her purse.

Oliver shut off another bank of lights. "I think that's the most sound business advice I've ever heard. When we took out that loan for the first tap house, I was sick for six months."

"Sizable loan?"

"More zeros than I'd ever seen. Although when we sold it, there were even more zeros," he grinned as he reached for the handle on the back door at the same time she did.

Their hands grazed, and Paige laughed as she looked up at him. His dark eyes were even darker in the shadows.

She pushed open the door and stepped out into the briskness of the early morning. "Do you guys think you'll ever sell this one?"

"Two years ago when we started to plan it, yes, that was the plan. Then Joel goes off and falls in love with the woman in pink next door, and well, I don't hear too much about selling anymore."

Paige laughed at the imagery of her sister as the woman in pink. Nothing summed up Kennedy more, she thought.

"Things worked out well for them."

Oliver shut the door and checked that it had locked behind him. "Married with a kid. Who would have thought?"

Paige wouldn't have guessed that would have happened after Kennedy had gotten so worked up about a bar going in next to her prissy shop.

They stood for a moment in awkward silence before Paige let out a breath. "Are you coming to class on Monday?"

"I'll be there."

"I guess I'll see you then," she said, feeling as if she should move in for a hug, but they weren't those kinds of friends.

"See you then."

Paige walked to her car, opened the door, and slid in behind the wheel as Oliver slowly walked to his truck.

She knew he wouldn't get in until she started her car and drove away. They'd spent enough time together that she knew he was nothing but a gentleman.

As she drove away, she waved, and watched him grow smaller in her rear view mirror. She let out another breath. When did she start finding Oliver Westcott to be so attractive?

CHAPTER 4

Wind chimes soothed as Paige sat on her mat in front of her class, her eyes closed. "Kiss your ear to your shoulder," she instructed in a soft tone. "Now to the other side."

She could hear the collective breath of the six people who had joined her that morning, and the one, she would call it a grunt, from the husband who had come with his wife for the first time.

"Gently roll your shoulders back." She did the move herself, her eyes still closed. "Now roll them forward."

Her early six o'clock class was her favorite because it got her blood moving for the day, and she knew her students had the same appreciation—except, perhaps, for the husband who still struggled in the back. Paige kept her composure when she'd hear his wife give him tips as to how to cross his legs, breathe, or to stop grunting so loud.

"Today is a gift," she said softly. "Set your intentions for the day, remembering that if things don't go as smoothly as you intend, you can come back to your mat, your office chair, or anywhere that brings you comfort, and breathe to find that stillness and calm you need to move forward. Take another deep breath in, lifting your arms over your head, pressing your palms together at the top and rest them at your third eye. Think of that intention that you've set for yourself and take another breath in through your nose and out through your mouth."

Paige listened to the breath move around her.

"Lower your hands from your third eye to your chest, and take a moment to check in with yourself. You've moved your body. You've set your intention for the day. Now take in one more breath." She inhaled and exhaled. "Open your eyes. Feel the peace that surrounds you and go forth with that in your heart. Namaste."

The class in front of her sat still for one more moment while everyone collected themselves and finished their breath. Then, as a collective unit, they all began their post class ritual of rolling their mats and talking in hushed tones.

Paige moved to the edge of the room and turned up the lights with the dimmer switch, just enough that everyone could see to gather their belongings.

As always, the volume of voices began to rise and conversations were started. When people gathered together so early in the morning to bring peace and calm into their lives, it tended to forge some friendships of the like-minded.

Paige's sister-in-law, Meghann, slipped her arms through her coat and picked up her yoga mat. "This is exactly what I needed before a long day of meetings," she said.

"That sounds horrible," Paige joked.

"It is, but the payoff will be fantastic. In January, I'll start filming a new show. Max is working with the production company to rent them the space in his old warehouse."

Paige thought about her brother and what he'd given up just to be with Meghann. Then she reconsidered. He'd sold off his well-established business for a great deal of money, but he'd kept the construction lot, offices, and the small warehouse. Now it seemed as if it were going to be put to good use.

"He hasn't gone stir crazy yet?"

Meghann laughed. "I would have thought he might by now, but he's having a good time remodeling the house."

"He enjoys that stuff. How's your mother?"

Meghann blew out a breath. "Yesterday she had a really hard day. Alzheimer's doesn't give you a schedule, that's for sure. She's had some good days lately, but when it's bad—it's bad."

Paige touched Meghann's arm and gave her a supportive smile. "I'm glad you're here for her."

"So am I. I'll see you on Wednesday," Meghann said as she leaned in and hugged Paige, then turned and walked out with a group of others that waved back.

As the room emptied, Paige noticed that Oliver was still seated on his mat quietly.

This was the kind of place she'd always hoped to create, a safe environment where a man felt comfortable enough to linger silently even when everyone else around him had moved on.

When she passed by him, she noticed he opened his eyes and looked up at her.

"I didn't mean to bother you," she said softly, and he smiled up at her.

"Just needed another moment."

"Take as many as you need."

Oliver ran his hand over his beard and then raked his fingers through his unruly hair. Paige found it charming that at six in the morning he wasn't molded together with hair product.

"I think I'm ready to face the day, though it's my day off. I might just go back to bed," he yawned.

"It's foggy out with a brisk chill. It's the kind of morning that warrants climbing back into bed. I'm grateful that this many of you join me this early in the morning."

"It puts my mind straight," Oliver admitted as he moved to his knees and began to roll up his mat. "One thing that was always part of my life, before and after I lived with my grandparents, was taking time to be mindful."

Paige moved to the shelf where she had her iPod set up and turned off the music. "How old were you when you went to live with your grandparents?"

Oliver tucked the mat under his arm and stood. "I was eight."

"So they raised you?"

"Yeah. Eight is still pretty young when you look back at it."

"It's very young. And why did you go live with them?" she asked turning to see him standing in the middle of the empty room.

"It was the right thing to do."

She wondered if she'd crossed a line, but then again, he had mentioned to her the other night that his mother had written him a letter. Maybe he needed to talk about it. Paige was no therapist, but she was more than willing to lend an ear when a friend needed it.

"If you're not really going to run home and go back to bed, we could go get some coffee. If you're up to it," she offered.

Oliver shrugged. "I could go with a cup of tea. I could also make you a cup of coffee, if you're up to it," he repeated what she'd said to him. "I have to feed the cat."

"You have a cat?"

"You don't like cats?"

"Just didn't know you were a cat person."

"I have a cat."

"I'll let you make me coffee," she said.

A smile formed on his lips and Paige decided it was the right thing to do—to have coffee or tea with the man to set his day straight.

CHAPTER 5

Paige followed the directions that her phone was giving her as she drove to Oliver's house. He'd left before Paige had, having texted her his address.

She found it amusing that in two years, she'd never been to his house. Oliver had attended her classes faithfully, and they'd even gone on day trips and hikes together, but they'd never been to each other's houses.

When she heard the words, "Your destination is on the right," she turned her head to see a small bungalow type house situated in the center of a row of similar looking houses. There was a bright yellow bicycle on the front porch, as well as a macramé plant holder with a bright pot, but obviously nothing growing in it during the October chill.

Paige pulled her car in front of the house, put it in park, and turned off the engine. Because there was a good share of vanity that ran through her veins, she flipped open the mirror on the back side of her visor, pulled out her shimmery Kennedy Pink lip gloss, and added a hit of color to her lips.

There wasn't much more she could do with the knot of hair on top of her head, but she was still in her yoga pants and tank top, so it went with the look. She'd thrown on an oversized sweatshirt, in lieu of a real jacket, to keep her warm.

Opening her door, she swung her feet out and reached back to pick up her phone as it began to ring. Her sister's face appeared on the screen.

"What's up, sis?" she answered as she climbed from the car.

"Where are you?"

"I'm having a coffee date after class. Do you need me?"

"Can you talk for a moment?"

Paige closed the car door and bumped it with her hip to ensure it closed. "Yeah."

"You worked later on Saturday after we left the tap house, right?"

"Yes," she drew out the word. "I was there until two-thirty."

She heard her sister let out a long breath. "Who closed out the cash drawer behind the bar?"

"Oliver."

"Right."

Paige leaned up against her car. "What's going on?"

"Just some discrepancies, and Joel wanted me to ask you who was around that night."

"Then ask me that," Paige snapped. "The way you're saying it, you're accusing Oliver."

"I didn't say that," Kennedy defended.

"Nope, but you didn't give me all the information either."

"Okay, who else was there?"

Paige thought back. "Craig."

Kennedy let out a low hum. "I'll let Joel know that too."

"Do you think they're stealing from each other? The four of them are tight. Why would one of them do that to the others?"

"I don't think they would."

"So maybe nothing is missing and there is a mathematical error."

"Maybe."

Paige didn't buy into her sister's middle of the road answer. "Listen, I have to go. Let me know what you find out."

"I will. Hey, sis," Kennedy said softly. "I love you."

"I love you too."

The call ended there and Paige gripped tightly to her phone as she turned to walk toward the house. Before she reached the front steps to the porch, the front door opened and Oliver smiled down at her.

He'd had time to fix his hair and throw on a different T-shirt. He looked more like the man she was used to seeing.

"Welcome to my abode," he said, holding the door open for her.

"Thanks." Paige stepped past him and into the small house.

"Something bothering you?" he asked as he shut the door behind her.

Paige turned to look at him, forcing a smile to her lips. "No. My sister just called. Sometimes it's a little much."

"Siblings, huh?"

Yeah, siblings, she thought.

"Come on in," Oliver offered as he started through the house.

Paige began to follow him, taking in the layout and the decor —or lack thereof.

They had walked into the living room, which had a TV, two recliners, and a bookshelf filled with books. She assumed that the alcove behind the living room was where a dining room table would go, but there was no furniture there. At the back of the living area there was another door, which wasn't closed completely, and she could see that it was his bedroom.

As she followed him to the kitchen, she noted there was another bedroom next to the small bathroom, but it was empty. The kitchen was tiny, but he had a small table pushed up against the wall with two chairs on either side of it. The cabinets appeared to be original to the house, and Paige had lived in the town long enough to know that the houses dated back to the forties.

"This is a cute house," she said as she pulled out one of the chairs and sat down.

"I like it. It's nostalgic."

"Haven't lived here very long, huh?"

Oliver turned back to her, a mug in each hand. He set one down in front of her, and the other in front of the empty chair. "Almost seven years," he said. "I realized I only had instant coffee. But I have assorted teas," he motioned to the box on the table.

"Tea is fine," Paige said pulling the box toward her to sort through his selection. "You're a minimalist."

Oliver sat down in the chair across from her. "Totally. Never had much. Don't see the need to bog myself down with a bunch of junk. I guess I always figured the less you had to carry, the quicker you could get out of town."

His answer was unsettling to her, and it shouldn't have been. Paige had been with Oliver when he'd closed out his drawer. He'd even done some kind of dance when it balanced, she remembered, and Craig had seen it too. The accusations they were making against him were wrong.

Then again, Kennedy hadn't directly made an accusation, she'd asked a question.

"Are you sure you're okay?" Oliver asked as he pulled a tea packet from the box. "You didn't have to come over if you have other things to do."

"Sorry. Just have something on my mind. So, where is your cat?"

As if the cat were trained to appear when asked for, it jumped up on Oliver's lap.

He eased back in his chair and stroked a hand over the cat's orange fur. "This is Blane," he said snuggling the cat.

"Blane?"

"You know, he's pompous. Blane is a pompous kind of name."

That warranted a laugh from Paige. "I suppose. How long have you had him?"

Oliver puckered his lips in thought. "Five years, or so. He showed up one day, and never left. I combed the area, but no one had lost him. I put out notices online, no one came. Animal control and the local vets had never seen him. So, I figured he was a pompous ass who moved in with me, and I named him Blane. We've been together ever since."

A man who took in stray cats and didn't have furniture or a coffee maker wasn't lifting money from his business partners.

Paige opened her tea bag and dunked it into the hot water in the mug. No, Oliver was a gentle spirit, but she'd known that.

CHAPTER 6

Oliver enjoyed Mondays. They started with the yoga class, and nothing else was expected of him. He put in his hours at the tap house, just like everyone else, but usually, they all respected the one day off each of them got.

He stood at the sink hand washing the two mugs he and Paige had used when she'd stopped for coffee—which turned into tea. Oliver enjoyed Paige's company, and had since the moment they'd met. They'd seemed to just hit it off.

In fact, he'd hit it off with all of Joel's new in-laws. And to think, when he'd first seen Joel's wife, Kennedy, he'd thought she was snobby. There had been nothing but her appearance to back that up, but it had been the first impression. Oliver couldn't have been more wrong.

The entire Devereaux clan was nothing but sincere and help-ful. They dove into helping at the tap house anytime it was needed, and for that, he was grateful. But there was more to it. They'd become his family too, and he'd never had that.

Oliver set the mugs in the drying rack and leaned against the counter. Usually, after yoga on Monday, he'd do just as he'd said he wanted to. He'd go home and climb back into bed. Now, he was wide awake and alone in his empty house.

He decided to go out to his garage and work out.

Oliver grabbed the key to the garage off the hook at the back door, and walked through his postage stamp sized yard to the detached garage. He pushed open the door, embracing the smell of the old garage that had seen many families come and go.

He flipped on the switch and took in the surroundings.

There was an old work bench that appeared to be as old as the garage itself. Perhaps the original owner, back in the forties, had used the space to build things or work on a monster of a car. Oliver amused himself wondering if an old Buick would fit in the small garage.

Oliver had repurposed the garage for a gym. He had a set of dumbbells, a ratty weight bench, a medicine ball, a TRX, and a rower. It was sad, but it served its purpose.

He turned on his speaker, found a playlist on his phone, and sat down on the rower. As was the norm, he began to row, and his mind wandered somewhere else.

Often this was the time he'd clear his head, but his mother's letter was constantly on his mind now. Why on earth, after twenty some years, did she decide she wanted to get in touch with him? Seriously, what did she have to offer him? What did she want from him?

Oliver picked up his pace, and his heart rate increased. The music on his phone was drowned out as his breathing increased.

There wasn't any part of him that wanted get in touch with his mother. She'd never come for him when he'd wanted her to. He saw no reason to engage now.

When he could no longer see, because the sweat had dripped into his eyes, he slowed his pace. It never seemed as if he'd rowed very long, but the distance would say differently.

Oliver climbed off the machine and sat down on the weight

bench. As often as he worked out in the garage, he didn't think it showed. Perhaps he wasn't too serious about it.

He picked up the dumbbells he'd left the last time he'd worked out. Twenty-five pounds apiece, today they felt as if they weighed one hundred. Nonetheless, he managed a few reps before he dropped them back to the floor.

Maybe a visit with his grandmother would calm him. She had a way of doing that.

OLIVER HAD SHOWERED, gelled his hair, and conditioned his beard. His grandmother loved his beard, and found great joy in giving it a little tug.

As he parked in front of the house in which he'd grown up, Oliver put the car in park, and turned off the engine. He took a moment to unroll his long sleeves and button the cuffs. His grandmother didn't approve of tattoos, and Oliver had successfully hidden his from her for nearly three years.

His grandmother was standing with the front door open the moment he stepped out of the car.

Her hair was a mass of gray curls atop her head, and she wore a gingham apron. Oliver was familiar with the aprons she'd made when she was first married. There was a different color for each day of the week, and a special one for Sundays.

"Ollie, I'm so happy to see you." Her voice warmed him, and he thought of the comfort in that.

"Hey, Gran." He hurried to her and kissed her on the cheek. "What are you baking?"

"Cinnamon rolls. I have a batch coming out of the oven. Can I interest you in one?"

He thought of the yoga class he'd taken that morning and the workout he'd completed. "I suppose I could spare a few calories."

His grandmother laughed. "You're perfectly fit. You can afford a cinnamon roll."

Oliver followed his grandmother to the kitchen and the smell filled his nose. When he thought of home, these were the kinds of things he thought of.

Since his grandfather's death, nearly ten years earlier, his grandmother kept busy at the local church, volunteering her time. Though her faith was solid, it wasn't something that comforted Oliver, and his grandmother had never pushed the issue with him.

"The ladies auxiliary is having a bake sale tomorrow. You should drop by and buy something," she suggested, but he knew it meant he needed to be there.

"I'll do my best. I work tomorrow evening."

"It starts at noon and goes until six. You can drop by."

With that, he knew that he'd show up right at noon and buy some brownies.

Oliver sat down at her table and his grandmother served him up a hot cinnamon roll. He smiled when he saw the glaze drip from the sides. As a child, that had been his favorite part to help with.

"So what's on your mind?" she asked as she sat down across from him.

"What makes you think..."

"You're my blood. There's something stirring in your head."

Oliver wasn't sure why he'd thought he could keep it from her. "Mom sent me a letter."

His grandmother's eyes widened and then her smile softened the look she gave. "She's coming around, huh?"

"Twenty years is too late." Oliver cut into the cinnamon roll. "Am I being petty?"

"Are you?"

Oliver chuckled. "No. I had a good life. She wasn't part of it. I'm doing just fine."

"Then I think you have your answer," his grandmother said as she stood to tend to the cinnamon rolls in the oven.

There hadn't been much to the conversation with his grandmother, but for some reason Oliver felt better just talking to her. No, it wasn't petty. He didn't have to have anything to do with his mother. His grandmother was his rock. His friends were his family. There was nothing missing in Oliver's life. For the moment, this pity party was over.

CHAPTER 7

Tuesdays and Thursdays were Paige's full days at the wellness center. She worked the front desk, and taught five different classes. The lunchtime class had ended, and she sat alone in the quiet space looking at numbers on her laptop. The spreadsheet she'd created to calculate what she needed to buy the center read like a coloring page. Black and red numbers in different columns presented themselves as times she'd been ahead and times she'd had to dip into her finances.

There'd be no way she'd ever admit how jealous she was at her siblings' successes, or the numbers in their bank accounts. Kennedy's average sale was nearly a thousand dollars. The clients she kept were well off and loved pretty things. Chase's limo business now boasted six cars, and the wait to get the big Hummer limo, used mostly for parties and such, was nearly four months long. Then there was Max. He'd sold off his construction company for a pretty penny when he married Meghann, who on her own, had come into a windfall of money when she'd been fired from her cooking show, they'd paid out her contract, and she'd picked up another. Kennedy's husband Joel and his partners, including Oliver, were steadily busy every night of the

31

week. They had honed in on what the small area of town had needed, and they were doing just fine.

Each one of them had offered to carry a loan for her, or buy in as a partner to the wellness center. But that wasn't what Paige wanted. She wanted to make it all on her own too. She supposed she could take her clientele and do classes from her living room, but that wasn't what she wanted. She wanted the whole package. The retail of essential oils and charms in the front, the yoga studio in the center, and the unoccupied rooms for massage. The business plan she'd drawn up in college for an assignment still was the plan she wanted to follow. But she was coming up short.

Paige had a month to make her final offer, or the owner would sell to someone else.

No blame was put on the current owner for making the stipulation. She wanted Paige to have it, but it'd been nearly a year since Paige had spoken to her about it. The time was now.

As she clicked out of the spreadsheet, she saw the open web browser with slides of Oahu, and she cringed. Maybe she just needed to tell her father that she couldn't make it to his wedding. It was at a very unfortunate time for her. To make the trip and give her classes to someone else to cover, was going to cost her dearly. He'd understand, wouldn't he?

Paige let out a breath. No. He wouldn't understand. Sure, he had three other children that would be there, but it wouldn't be the same if she wasn't there. It would be as if she was shunning him.

He'd been her only parent since she was seven, and he'd taken that responsibility very seriously. She couldn't let him down when he'd finally found someone who made him as happy as she could remember her mother making him.

Paige closed the laptop and batted back tears.

Maybe, just maybe, she'd have to borrow the money.

When the door opened, Paige jumped. She didn't have

another class until two, so she hadn't expected anyone to walk in. But she smiled when she saw Oliver walk through the door.

"You busy?" he asked.

"No. Are you headed to work?"

He nodded. "Do you like brownies?"

The smile faded from her lips and her stomach instantly growled. "Yes."

"You don't look like it entices you."

"Wrong. It entices me too much. Why do you have brownies?"

He set the plate he carried in on the counter. "My grandma and the church ladies were having a bake sale and I'd promised her I'd come by. I bought three plates of brownies, a box of cupcakes, and a cake."

Paige laughed. "And what are you going to do with all of that?"

"Oh, it's as good as gone. I'll take it to work with me and you won't see a crumb of it by five o'clock."

"No doubt. What truck is there tonight?" Paige asked slipping her fingers under the wrap on the plate and breaking off a small piece of brownie.

Oliver pursed his lips. "I think it's the fish taco truck."

Paige considered it as she popped the small bite of brownie in her mouth, and realized that she was going to eat the entire plate of brownies before her next class if he left them.

"Maybe I'll make that dinner," she said, licking a crumb off of her finger.

"About six?"

"Closer to seven. I have a class at six."

"Right. The after work crowd."

She laughed. "Right. Then tonight is my eight o'clock beginners class too."

"It keeps you busy."

"Just wish it brought in more money," she admitted as she

lifted the cover off the plate again, and this time took a full brownie.

Oliver leaned against the counter, propping his elbows on it. "I'm still in if you are looking for a business partner," he said and Paige bit into the brownie.

"I don't want a partner. I want to do it myself."

"But you're worried about it."

She set the brownie down. "I am worried. And you, my sister, my sister-in-law, and both of my brothers have offered to help me. But if I can't raise the money on my own, then maybe it's not worth it, right?"

Oliver shrugged. "The four of us put everything on the line when we decided to open the first tap house. I've never been more sick in all my life. But ya know, when you have to make it work, it works."

"And look at your house. You don't even have furniture. Why don't you buy things if you're doing okay?"

Oliver chuckled. "That's what you saw when you came to my house? Lack of furniture?"

Paige let her shoulders drop. "You know what? That was rude of me. I'm sorry."

"Don't be sorry. I'm doing okay. I own that little house. Lock, stock, and barrel. I'm thirty. That's pretty good if you ask me."

"It is good. Again, it was rude."

"Nah, people are caught up on possessions. I wasn't raised like that. I didn't own a pair of shoes until I was seven," he said and Paige felt the air clog her lungs.

"Seriously?"

"Seriously. I didn't have conventional toys, or a bathroom. I lived in a park in a teepee that got moved a lot when the cops would come and break up all of those living there."

Paige reached a hand out and touched his arm. "You were homeless?"

Oliver chuckled again. "Or free, as my parents put it."

She was beginning to understand. "Where was this?"

"San Fran. Not all the hippies moved out in the seventies."

And didn't that shed some new light on the man? As he pushed himself back from the counter, she saw his tattoo peek out from under his rolled sleeve.

"Your tattoo. I noticed it the other day."

Oliver pushed up his sleeve. "My grandmother has never seen it. I try to keep it from her, but one of these days, I'm going to forget and I'll hear about it."

"It's a teepee and a compass." She understood it now.

"Something to always remember where I came from," he said looking down at this forearm. "Good or bad, you're planted and then you grow."

"Wow, profound."

Oliver shrugged. "Then I was replanted here with my grand-parents and I flourished. The sun shines a little different here," he said with a wink. "I have to go. I'll see you when you come over."

With that, Oliver smiled and gave her a little wave as he walked out the door. The sun shines a little different here, she replayed his words in her head. After her mom was killed, Kennedy and Chase replanted themselves at her house, and they'd all flourished, she supposed.

Letting out a breath, she broke off another piece of brownie and popped it into her mouth. Her mind wandered back to the conversation she'd had with her sister about the cash drawer being mishandled. How could someone as clear minded as Oliver have done that? He certainly didn't need it, and obviously had too much respect for everyone and everything around him.

Covering up the plate of brownies, Paige tucked them under the counter, opened her laptop, and went back to depressing herself over her own finances.

CHAPTER 8

O liver tied on his apron as he whistled. Then he picked up the cake and the plates of treats and carried them behind the bar.

"What's all this?" Craig asked.

"My grandmother made me go to her bake sale. Take any of it you want."

He watched Craig lift the covering and pull out a brownie. "Damn," he said smoothly as he took a bite and let it melt in his mouth. "There's nothing like a homemade brownie."

"When does the truck get here?"

Craig licked his fingers. "It was supposed to be here at noon. It's late."

"We called?"

"Joel is in the office, talking to the guy now."

Oliver thought he'd get more information, and took a plate of brownies to the office. He could hear Joel finish his conversation as he opened the door.

"Food truck is a no show?" he asked and Joel raised his head. He wasn't sure, but it looked as if he'd been sized up by his friend.

"Blown tire. He'll be here in the next hour or so."

"Good. I have a dinner date," Oliver joked and set the plate on the desk. "My grandmother and her church ladies had a bake sale. Eat up."

Joel looked at the plate and then back up at Oliver. "Do you have a minute?"

Oliver nodded, and pulled his hand over his beard. "Of course. What's up?"

Joel stood and shut the door before motioning to Oliver to take a seat.

It was rather formal, Oliver thought, but he sat down across from Joel.

"Listen, I'm not accusing, but are you doing okay?"

Oliver leaned back in the chair and ran his hand over his beard again, something he did when he needed a moment to think.

"I'm doing great."

Joel nodded his head slowly. "I'm not going to beat around the bush. We have money missing, and it's been happening on your shifts."

Oliver felt the blood drain from his face, and then return hot and fiery. "I beg your pardon."

"Facts, man. That's all."

"Facts. You think I would do that to my partners? I would screw you all over?"

"I don't want to think that."

"But you do. You think I'm stealing."

"I think that the bookkeeper says it's on your shifts. That's what I'm saying."

"I'm not the only person that works my shifts."

"Craig and Paige were with you the other night," Joel said. "Which one of them should I talk to next?"

Oliver clasped his hands together and wrung his fingers. "Either one of them. You know, your sister-in-law is hard up for money." The moment the words were out of his mouth he could feel the vileness of them and it choked him. "Shit. I didn't mean that. She wouldn't do that—ever. But neither would I."

Joel let it sit on the air for a moment. "I don't think you would either."

Oliver felt the room cool a bit as he defused. "Okay, then. So, we have a leak somewhere."

"Consistent with when you're here."

"I don't like that."

"I don't either," Joel confirmed. "We need to find it."

Oliver sat silent, looking at his friend of almost a decade. He never would have gone into a business with someone if he didn't think they were true to their word. Never had he known Joel or his brother Jeff to be anything but truthful, hardworking men. Craig, he was the newest of their partners, but it had been Oliver that had brought him into the circle, and he, too, was an honest man.

All of this news twisted in Oliver's gut. "We'll figure this out, man. Maybe it was a clerical error."

"Maybe," Joel agreed. "If anything comes to mind that might have been missed, let me know."

"You'll be the first," Oliver agreed, and in a sign of good faith, reached his hand across the desk and shook Joel's.

THE TAP HOUSE wasn't too busy when Paige walked in just past seven. She'd eaten more brownies than she'd wanted to, and had decided to leave the tray out for after her last class. Luckily, everyone had eaten them. But she was in need of food before her next class, and thankfully the fish taco truck had a grilled shrimp option that didn't fill her up too much.

Oliver was behind the bar. His eyes met hers, but they were shrouded with worry. What could upset him in the past few hours that would leave his eyes so dark?

Then Paige remembered the conversation she'd had with her

sister about the money in the drawer. Maybe that had something to do with it.

"Hey, not too busy tonight," she said sliding onto one of the bar stools.

"All the better."

"Something wrong?" Paige asked as Oliver walked around the bar.

"Let's get some food. I'll let you in on it," he said leaving Craig behind the bar.

They walked outside to where the truck was set up. Paige had ordered from this truck every week for over a year, yet she always liked to look at the menu. She ordered her grilled shrimp tacos, and Oliver did the same. When she went to pay, he waved her off.

"They were late and said we eat free," he told her, so she dropped the money in her hand into the tip cup.

Heaters were scattered on the patio next to the large wooden picnic tables. Paige followed Oliver to a table and sat down across from him.

"There are those nights when I know I have one more class to teach, but I'd rather go home and watch TV," Paige admitted as she squeezed her lime over her tacos.

"Not feeling it tonight?" Oliver asked as he picked up a taco and took a bite.

"That trip to Hawaii is weighing heavily on my mind." Oliver only nodded in response. "Do you have something on your mind?" she asked and his eyes stayed averted until after he'd taken another bite from his taco.

"Seems as if there has been some money going missing, and it only happens on my shift."

Paige picked up her napkin and wiped her mouth. "Kennedy said something about it."

"Oh, so this is family gossip?" he snipped.

"I suppose she mentioned it because I was working too."

Oliver pushed his food boat away. "I didn't take anything."

"I believe you."

"Good, then convince your family."

Paige pushed her food boat to the center of the table as well. "If you didn't do anything, then you have nothing to worry about."

Oliver ran his hand over his beard. "You're right. I didn't do anything and Joel only asked. It's not as if he was nasty about it. I just have to watch what happens from here on."

"Maybe it was a transposed number or a bookkeeping error."

"Only if my luck should change. Sorry I got upset about your family."

"They're my family. I totally understand how you can get upset over them." Paige pulled her boat back toward her and picked up her taco. She believed that Oliver hadn't done anything wrong. If her family pushed too hard, she'd step in.

CHAPTER 9

There had been no more talk of missing money for the rest of the week, and Oliver decided that maybe it had been a mistake, and they'd just pushed on, which was what they should have done. He hadn't lifted any money, and he'd never do such a thing.

When he arrived at the tap house at noon, he was in full costume for the Halloween crowd.

Joel was the first to see him and smiled wide. "Captain Jack Sparrow, it's good to see you, mate!" He reached out his hand and shook Oliver's, pulling him in for a manly hug.

There was comfort in the gesture, as that was how they were usually around one another.

"And you are?" Oliver scanned a look over his friend who stood before him in a pair of jeans and a polo shirt with the tap house name on the chest.

"An asshole for not showing up looking like you," Joel laughed. "Kennedy is coming in at four and has a couples' costume for us. My mom is keeping the baby for the night."

"Can't wait to see what it is."

"Me either, though I'm extremely worried I'll be some cartoon character."

The very thought humored Oliver as he walked to the back room and pulled his apron from the peg.

For a night like Halloween, it was all hands on deck. The four partners would be there, any spouses that came with the partners, and their usual staff. Paige had agreed to bus tables all night as well.

The thought of Paige in a costume had the corners of Oliver's mouth turning up. Would she be a sexy cat? A sexy nurse? A sexy character from Harry Potter?

He felt the flush in his cheeks. She'd been on his mind a lot the past week. They'd spent a lot more time talking, he supposed, and he enjoyed it. Then again, he'd always enjoyed Paige's company. Over the past two years they'd become friends. She was the kind of person to take interest in someone, and she'd made him open up more than most people could. She wasn't hard on the eyes either.

Oliver chuckled to himself, and then caught sight of himself in the small mirror in the back room. At that point, his chuckle turned into a full laugh. He'd accentuated his beard with little charms in lieu of small braids, but he didn't think it detracted from the look. It was the hat and hair that brought it all together, though, he wasn't sure how long he could have that synthetic mop on his head.

Jeff walked through the back door and immediately smiled when he saw Oliver.

"Epic," was all he said as he passed by in a baseball jersey that said Ruth on the back.

It was going to be a fun night, Oliver decided.

PAIGE WONDERED if she should have arrived before five o'clock when she walked through the back door of the tap house, having had to park three blocks away. There were wall-to-wall people, all in costume.

When she saw her sister and brother-in-law, she busted into laughter.

Kennedy turned to her. "You're going to freeze," she said to Paige as she scanned a look over her.

"Just my stomach," she said leaning in and kissing Kennedy on the cheek. "Wilma?"

"You saw my Fred, right?"

Paige nodded and laughed. "Is he mad?"

"He'll be fine. He assumed he'd be some cartoon character. Now you have to see Hillary and Chase?"

"Please tell me they're Barney and Betty."

Kennedy raised her brows and Paige knew she'd hit the nail on the head.

Paige made her way through the crowd to the bar and squeezed her way in between two sexy cats there were talking up Captain Jack.

It took her a moment to realize it was Oliver, and boy, didn't he look sexy as a grungy pirate?

"Hey, sailor. You in town for a while?" she joked and watched as he turned to her, a smile on his lips, and then his eyes scanned over her.

"Wow," was all he said.

Paige spun in a slow circle, just as a real belly dancer would, making sure to engage all the charms on her outfit so that they made their own music.

"Can you really belly dance?" he asked, and she thought he might have choked a little on the words.

Because she was feeling playful, she stepped closer to him. "I can. But I charge for private dances," she laughed and picked up a tray, skirting around Oliver and out from behind the bar.

The little exchange had heated her, and she wasn't sure what to do with that feeling. In the past few weeks, she'd spent more time with him than she had the past few years. They'd always been friendly. They'd even gone on a few hikes and had a few meals. But she was seeing him differently now.

Paige moved toward a table with empty glasses and began to load them on her tray. When she looked up toward the bar, she noticed his eyes were on her. He smiled, as if he realized he'd been caught looking.

It was going to be an interesting night.

As she moved to the next table, she saw her brother walk by dressed as Barney, and she couldn't help but bust into a laugh.

"Oh my God! Hillary can convince you to do anything, can't she?"

Chase narrowed his eyes on her. "Max is dressed as DiMaggio and Meghann is Monroe. DiMaggio wears a suit. Max is in a damn suit and I'm dressed like this."

Paige moved in toward him to kiss him on the cheek. "This says true love, brother. You're an amazing husband for doing it."

"She could have convinced me to wear a trash bag," he admitted.

"She could convince you to do anything. Hell, you're married and have a kid," Paige reminded him.

"Like you said, its true love. Marriage and family were exactly what were missing from my life."

Someone called his name and Chase turned and walked away.

Marriage and family were exactly what were missing from my life. The words played again in her head.

A pang of jealousy surfaced before she could push it down. Her siblings were much older than she was. They'd done all the things she was just now getting the chance at. Business. Family. She wanted it all now.

Her eyes wandered back toward the bar and the man that served beers from behind it. Was that why she was finding him so attractive? Was her biological clock ticking?

Perhaps she needed to be very aware of that fact. Focusing on such details would only derail her plans.

CHAPTER 10

It was three o'clock in the morning. Kennedy was curled up on a bench, her head rested against the wall, and she was asleep. Joel sat next to her, his eyes batting open and closed as he tried to stay awake.

Hillary rubbed her eyes as Chase finished his bottle of water.

Max and Meghann had left as soon as the bar was cleaned up, and Paige wondered why she hadn't run out with them.

Oliver pulled the small accent clips out of his beard and tossed them into the pirate hat which sat on the chair next to him.

"I'm exhausted," he said and Joel groaned his agreement.

"Epic night," Craig said as he and Jeff emerged from the office. "We broke records with this one."

"Good," Joel mumbled. "At least it was worth it."

Oliver ran his fingers through his hair. "Football game in—" he checked his watch, "ten hours."

Jeff chuckled. "You'd better get home and get some sleep then. You're opening."

Oliver let out a long breath and stood. "I'll be getting gone, then."

Paige watched him pick up the hat from the other chair, and decided she needed to head home too. "I guess I'll head out too. I have to hike to my car," she humored.

"I'll give you a ride," Oliver offered.

"It's only three blocks."

"It's only three in the morning."

He was a gentleman, and she appreciated that.

They said goodbye to everyone and walked out the back door to where Oliver's Prius waited. He opened the passenger door and Paige slid in as he walked around to the other side.

"Where's your car?"

"Northside Drive."

"That's more than three blocks."

"Six?"

"Maybe," he laughed as he started the car. "Thanks for helping out tonight. We sure needed everyone."

"It was fun. I cleaned up on the tip share too," she laughed knowing they all had. "Will you be okay to be here in the morning. I mean, aren't you exhausted?"

Oliver shrugged. "That's what it's about, right? I'm living the dream for a single guy. The dads get to sleep in. I get to go to work. I have a little time. I don't have to be here until eleven."

"I'd be happy to come and help."

"I won't need help. We won't be as busy as we were tonight. But if you'd like to come down, I'd love to have you hang out at the bar. Let's see," he thought for a moment. "Wing truck is there tomorrow."

She thought about it. "I could do chicken."

"You'll come?"

"I'll be there," she agreed remembering that she was going to finalize her Hawaii trip and make class plans. But that could all be done in the afternoon.

Oliver turned down Northside Drive, which at three in the

morning was empty. He pulled up to Paige's car and parked bumper to bumper.

"Thanks for the lift," Paige said as she fished her keys from her purse.

"Thanks for the help tonight."

"Least I could do for Captain Jack," she said laughing, lifting her eyes to his in the glow of his dash lights.

There was a moment of hesitation, and Paige leaned in toward him. He felt his breath catch, what was she doing? Oliver's lips parted. She was moving in to kiss him, he thought.

Then she pulled a clip from his beard. "You missed one," she said, now only an inch from him.

Oliver let his breath out slow and steady, so he didn't let on just how worked up she'd gotten him at that moment.

He reached to take the clip from her fingers. "Thank you," he said, but she hadn't moved back.

Now what?

Paige bit down on her bottom lip, and he felt his heart rate increase.

"I guess I should go," she said, but she didn't move.

"Right. I have to get home and come back," Oliver reminded them both.

Still, Paige didn't ease back.

"Are you going to make me do this?" she asked, her breath heavy now.

Oliver swallowed. "What are you going to do?"

She lifted a brow. "I was going to kiss you, but..."

Dear Lord, she was going to kiss him. Was he ready for that? Hell yeah he was, he thought as he lifted his hand to her cheek and pulled her toward him.

The moment their lips met, he swore he heard a sizzle from the heat that had been building between them. Paige leaned in closer, and a moment later she toppled over the center console and right into his lap, hitting her head on the window.

"God, are you okay?"

She laughed, rubbing her head in the confines of the driver's side of his car. "I'm fine. I guess for being a yoga teacher, I lack finesse."

"I think you did just fine," he eased his hand to her cheek and brought her back to his lips.

The awkward part was over, he decided when he took her mouth. The ice had been broken, and now this moment that had been building between them was happening.

Paige's chilled fingers came to the sides of his neck as her mouth opened to his. She tasted of beer and the chocolate she'd indulged in during the night. It was intoxicating.

As their kiss lingered, Paige moved so that she was straddling him. A Prius wasn't the car to make out in, Oliver thought as his hands came to her waist, and she flinched when his cold fingers touched her bare skin.

Paige eased back and sucked in a breath. "It might be too cold to do this here," she said laughing as their breath carried on the air and the windows steamed.

"A little tight too."

She lowered again and took his mouth one last time, pressing her body to his, no doubt feeling his arousal having her that close to him.

When she pulled back again, she held his face in her hands. "I think that's been building a long time."

All Oliver could do was nod, and feel the disappointment as Paige slid from his lap to the other seat.

"You need to get home," she said. "I'll come back later and hang at the bar. Maybe I'll bring my laptop and do my class plans there."

Again, he nodded.

"Good night," Paige whispered as she opened the car door and stepped out into the brisk air.

Oliver watched as she unlocked her car and started it. She sat for a few moments and eventually drove off.

He continued to sit in his car as the heater whirled warm air around him.

What did that just start, he wondered.

He'd have to do a lot of thinking on it. It wouldn't be long before she found out that things usually didn't work out for him, especially in the romance department.

CHAPTER 11

The smile was still on Paige's lips when she pushed open her front door, walked into her dark house, and closed it behind her. Before she even turned on the light, she leaned against the door and let out a long, slow breath.

Oliver had been on her mind a lot in the past few weeks. Oh, who was she kidding? The minute she met the man, when he and his business partners had begun their transformation of the building next to her sister's boutique, she'd been smitten. Initially, she didn't give much thought about her attraction to him. He was a good-looking man. She was a single woman. Attraction happened.

When her sister began a romance with his business partner Joel, then it seemed as if the men of the tap house were off limits. But she and Oliver remained friendly, having a few meals and going on outings.

When the flutter in her stomach eased a bit, she wondered if that was why he was ever present in her yoga classes. On a laugh, she pushed away from the door and turned on the light.

She'd have known if he had just wanted to be near her. Men didn't just dive into yoga and present the kind of flexibility and coordination that Oliver had. No, he was familiar with the practice, and was an ideal student.

Paige walked through the kitchen, pulled a glass from the cupboard, and filled it with water. As she sipped it, she looked at the clock on the microwave. It was past four o'clock in the morning. Her body was drained of energy, though the kiss she'd shared with Oliver had given it a jolt. Each of her limbs felt heavy as she walked down the hallway toward her bedroom.

Without flipping on the light, Paige set down her glass of water, stripped off the costume she'd donned for the evening, and climbed into her bed. The sheets were cool against her skin as she pulled them up to her chin and laid her head on the pillow.

Tomorrow, or later in the day, would be interesting. She'd taken initiative on a feeling that had been building for a long time. What would it change?

Had she simply kissed a man, and he reacted? Was he interested? Would this end up with them in bed, and nothing more? Or would she be the last of the Devereauxs to find love?

Laying in the dark with her eyes open, staring at the ceiling, she wondered if that was what she wanted. The frustration that surged through her over her father's wedding made her second guess ever wanting to actually get married. Didn't marriage and children interrupt the flow of life, not only the couple's but those around the couple as well?

That was petty. As she rolled to her side, she was irritated with herself for thinking that. One of the things she enjoyed more than anything was babysitting her nieces. They were the light in her life. So her father wanted a destination wedding. Why did that have to upset her? He deserved to celebrate his marriage to a woman he loved. He'd gone a long time without having that, after Paige's mother had tragically died.

Her mind wandered from family and new relationships to the pending purchase of the wellness center. All along, she'd said she wanted to do it on her own. She wanted to raise the money by working hard to buy the center, but didn't it come down to the fact that she didn't want to burden anyone?

Kennedy had loaned Chase money to purchase his house after he'd lost his finance job. Instead, Chase had put that money into a new limousine. Sure, it worked out, but Kennedy was furious. Max had once lent him money too, and all he and Kennedy could do for a while was talk about how irresponsible Chase was with their money.

Paige didn't want that. But time was ticking away, and if she didn't act on it soon, she wouldn't have the opportunity.

She rolled to her other side, pounded her pillow into place, and adjusted the sheets around her body. Perhaps Oliver would be the right person to ask for the money. He'd offered. And, after she'd seen his house, she knew he didn't want for anything. Maybe it wouldn't cause him any hardship to lend it to her.

But, if they got involved, that would make it a sticky situation. She didn't want to owe someone she was involved with. Nor did she want him to think she only got involved with him because she needed money.

Rolling onto her back, she stared up at the ceiling. This was why she wanted to fund the purchase herself.

Then, she laughed in the darkness. How had she gone from her body buzzing over a kiss with a man she found attractive, to wanting to borrow money from him, to worrying about relationships?

She needed a good night's sleep, and she wasn't sure she was going to get it now.

Paige sat up, kicked her legs over the edge of the bed, and picked up her robe from the floor. She shrugged it on, and walked to the kitchen.

On nights when she couldn't sleep, she made tea to calm herself. It wasn't just the herbal delight, but the process that brought calm to her.

It was a ritual that had started with Kennedy after Paige's mother had died, and she'd stopped sleeping.

There was comfort in thinking about her sister, her mother, the process, the tea, and the calm.

As she filled the kettle and set it on the stove, she wondered if Oliver had fallen into bed and was fast asleep. Had his grandmother offered him the same kind of support as Kennedy had offered her when her childhood was disrupted?

Paige leaned against the counter.

They were alike in that way, she and Oliver. His parents had been ripped from him, just as her mother had been ripped from her. Though, twenty-some years later, she'd never get a letter from her mother.

Was Oliver looking for comfort, too, when he returned the kiss she'd planted on him?

Now her mind stirred even more as the kettle began to whir next to her. Perhaps she wasn't going to get any sleep at all.

CHAPTER 12

The sound of the door latching behind Oliver as he'd pushed it closed, echoed through the house. Clapping his hands to turn on the side table lamp, he looked around. Wasn't it funny that the first thing Paige had noticed was how empty the place was.

Oliver dropped his keys in a bowl he kept on the half wall by the front door and walked inside, pulling off his coat, and draping it over the arm of the chair in the living room.

The lack of items in his house gave him peace. Yes, that's what it was. Nothing was out of place because there was nothing to leave out. There had been more once, he remembered as he ran his hand over the back of his neck while he walked to the kitchen and flipped the light switch.

When he'd graduated from college and landed his first job, he'd bought nice things to fill the holes in his life. One by one, those items walked away with women he brought home, or he'd smashed some of them against the walls in bouts of rage when he thought the path he'd chosen for his life was the wrong one.

The greatest thing he'd ever done for himself was take his ass to counseling, start doing yoga, and selling off the rest of his belongings. There was peace in the empty house. It had been years since he'd thrown anything at the wall, and nearly as long since he'd brought home a random stranger that walked away with something.

Pulling a glass down from the cupboard, Oliver filled it with water from the sink, and drank it down. It had been a long night —fun, but long. And it ended on a high that he hadn't felt in a very long time.

Oliver walked back to the living room and turned on the television as he passed by it to collect the mail that had collected through the mail slot and piled on the wall by the door. He hadn't sorted through it in a few days. The Oliver of the past might let that pile sit for weeks, but now that he was a financially stable business owner, he tended to it more regularly. No bills were ever late, and his checking account was always balanced to the penny.

An old episode of I Love Lucy started after the commercial break concluded, and Oliver stopped to watch Lucy scrunch up her nose as Ricky narrowed his eyes on her. Oliver laughed at the antics he'd watched on TV through his youth. His grandparents loved the black and white shows of the past, and he had a fond appreciation for them.

Plopping himself down into one of the oversized recliners that were the centerpiece of his living room, he set his glass of water on the small table to the side by the lamp and began to sort through the stack of mail.

Blane emerged from the shadows and wound around Oliver's feet before leaping up into the chair to nuzzle himself next to Oliver in the oversized chair.

"How was your night?" Oliver asked as he ran his hand over the cat's head and smiled as he purred. "Yeah, mine got interesting too. Man, did it get interesting."

Blane curled up next to him, settling in.

Oliver sorted through the mail that still rested on his lap. A water bill, six restaurant menus, an offer for funding, and two envelopes that he knew were birthday cards.

The one was scented, and it brought a smile to his lips when he saw his grandmother's handwriting. When he opened the card, a five dollar bill fell out, and he chuckled.

His entire life his grandmother sent him a birthday card with five dollars in it, even when he lived in her house a card would come in the mail. When he was a little boy, sometimes he would get two or three cards, depending on how long it took his grandmother to find them to get a card to him. It surprised him he could remember back that far, but he did.

Now that he'd lived on his own for almost twelve years, the card that arrived, always a few days before his birthday, brought him joy. He'd see his grandmother on his birthday, as it was their tradition to have breakfast together, but she'd still always send the card.

The next card had his name on it, but there was no return address, and the handwriting was shaky, much like his grandmother's had become.

Oliver ripped into the envelope and pulled out the card. There was a dinosaur on the front, and he smiled, but when he opened it, the humor was lost.

The inside of the card was filled with writing, which he didn't read first. His eyes went directly to the bottom of the card where it was signed, Mom.

Oliver closed the card, set the pile of mail on the table next to him, and drank down his water. Blane must have felt him tense because he uncurled himself from his place on the oversized chair and crawled up into Oliver's lap and settled in.

"You have my back, don't you?"

Closing his eyes, Oliver tried to clear his mind and take control of his breath. He needed to read what was in the card, he knew that. However, he'd been well-trained to find calm first before diving into a situation that might upset him.

Stroking his hand over his cat, and feeling his body move with his breath, calmed him. Nothing was going to change in that card before he got a good night's sleep. In the morning he'd go for a walk, whenever he woke up, work out, have some breakfast, and then maybe, just maybe, he'd read the card.

Picking the cat up in his arms, Oliver stood, turned off the television, and headed to the bedroom. When he'd returned home, his body had been buzzing from the kiss that Paige had planted on him. The thought distracted him as he set the cat on the bed.

As he undressed, he replayed the kiss in his head. Yes, he'd focus on that as he fell into bed. There would be no more thinking about his mother's note in the birthday card. He'd only think of Paige.

CHAPTER 13

P aige studied the computer screen and the itinerary for her pending trip to Hawaii. Her hesitation to book the flight had caused her to pay more when the prices went up, and if she didn't finalize her plans, she'd never be able to afford the trip.

She clicked the other tab on the screen and checked her bank account balance. Well, it was going to hurt, but she was going to focus on the joy of the time away, the beach, the sun, and time with her family.

Paige clicked back to the other tab and finalized her trip. The moment it began to process her payment, her stomach tightened. God, she was going to be sick. A week away from work and a hit to her finances, it was enough to send her to bed to recover.

Closing her laptop, she looked at the clock on her desk. It was nearly one o'clock in the afternoon. Where had the day gone? The truth was, she'd slept most of it away, but dreams about kissing Oliver had her wanting to stay in bed dreaming.

She'd told him she'd hang out with him while he worked. If she was going to keep her word, she needed to take a shower and head toward the tap house.

As she walked through the house, taking her hair out of the makeshift bun atop her head, she wondered if it was going to be awkward to see him after last night.

Paige had shifted the balance, and he'd been as interested in that shift.

Closing the bathroom door, Paige started the shower, and pulled off her clothes. What happened now, she wondered? Did they act like nothing happened? Would they sneak kisses for a while until they decided what they were doing? Would they build a relationship out of it, or would he act like nothing had happened? How was she supposed to know what to expect?

Stepping into the stream of water, she realized she'd forgotten to turn the knob up enough to trigger any warmth. She squealed as she tried to pull herself from the cold stream of water that pelted her skin. Maneuvering herself against the wall, she adjusted the temperature until the water warmed, and she could feel her muscles release.

That was a harsh reality, she laughed to herself. It was proof that her mind was elsewhere, and that was what happened when she got involved with a guy.

As she tipped her head back into the warm stream, she cleared her mind and decided she wasn't involved with anyone. Her only lover right now was her yoga school—or the dream of the school. That airline ticket and hotel reservation put a hole in her plans, but she had to remember that everything came to her if she worked hard enough. Maybe not right when she wanted it, but when she could handle it.

Maybe this thing with Oliver was the same way. She'd understand what they started when she could handle it.

OLIVER'S ATTENTION was on the television screen. Green Bay was going to win the game, and he was going to lose five bucks to the guy at the end of the bar working his way through his second flight of drinks.

He hadn't even noticed Paige walk through the door until he heard her voice as she said hello to Kendra who was washing glasses behind the bar.

Oliver turned to look at her, and he felt that jolt of uncertainty as they both laid eyes on one another for the first time since they'd kissed.

"Hey," he said, and cringed at how impersonal it seemed.

"Hey," she replied, obviously as uncertain as he was. "Do you guys have some coffee made?"

Oliver nodded. "Of course we do. The rule is, if Craig might stop by, and that's always, we have to have coffee brewed," he chuckled at his own joke and turned for a coffee mug. "Dragging today?"

Paige hopped up on a stool. "Yeah. I don't think I actually fell asleep until five this morning. And then I made my reservations for Hawaii, and that ate up a chunk of my savings. So I'm a little out of sorts."

Oliver poured coffee into the mug and thought that things had warmed up between them as Paige spoke of her morning. This was normal banter for them.

"That bad?" he asked as he set the mug in front of her.

"Thanks." She pulled the mug toward her. "Since I didn't make my reservations last week, the prices went up."

"You could just tell your dad you can't make it."

Paige shook her head and blew on the coffee. "I would never do that. He has always been there for me. I wouldn't think of not being there for him."

"So, the yoga studio has to wait longer?"

"I guess so. I'm not getting ahead as quickly as I'd wanted to."

Oliver leaned his elbows on the bar, and eased toward her. To capture her full attention, he took her hands and held them in his.

The shock that lit in her eyes worried him a bit. After the kiss they'd shared, he'd have thought this might be an understood gesture, but maybe he was wrong.

He didn't let go. Instead, he brushed his thumb over her knuckles.

"You've seen my house, and we've discussed how material things don't matter to me. I don't need for anything, and my savings account is well padded."

"Oliver..." she began to protest, and he gave her hands a gentle squeeze.

"I'll show you my books if you'd like."

Paige let out a small laugh. "I don't want to owe anyone."

"It's not that much money. You're not buying the building, you're taking over a clientele and a lease. You need enough to build the business you're buying and maybe do some updating."

"But what if it fails?"

"But what if it doesn't?"

"I don't want to owe anyone—ever."

"Then I guess your plans are on hold." He eased back slightly, but kept hold of her hands. "But, even if it failed, I could survive. I'm trying to tell you that I'd like to invest in your business. Finance only. When you pay it back, I'd be out of your hair all together."

"If it fails, I won't have anything to pay you back with."

"And that's the chance I would take to invest in your dream, Paige. Think about it. Why work as hard as I do if I can't help a friend?"

"Friend?"

"Are you?"

"Yeah," she said, on a disappointed sigh.

"Maybe that will grow into something bigger too," he offered, and he noticed that the shock in her eyes teetered between fear and flirtatiousness now.

"That would be mixing business and pleasure then. Wouldn't that be a mistake too?"

Oh, she was a doubtful one. "You're not the gambling sort, are you?"

"I have never been. I like to know where everything stands at all times."

"Maybe we should talk about what happened last night then," Oliver offered as the front door to the tap house opened and group of people walked in the door. "Why don't you go get some lunch. Order me something too. They have buffalo cauliflower."

Paige hopped off the stool. "Ranch or blue cheese?"

"Ranch. And lots of napkins," he called out after her as she walked away.

Oliver took the orders from the new patrons and turned to fill them. Watching the amber liquid fill each glass he thought about just how much of a gambling man he was. There was a wager to everything he ever did. Perhaps it wasn't gambling, it was just knowing that the odds were never in his favor and never had been.

But Paige was a gamble he was willing to take, both with his money and his heart.

CHAPTER 14

A hand rested on Paige's shoulder as she stood waiting for her food order. When she turned to see who had touched her, she saw her brother Chase smiling down at her.

"Having some lunch, little sis?"

"That or I'm standing in a random line for no reason."

Chase chuckled as he studied the menu, which she was sure he knew by heart by now. The wing truck was always a favorite among the Devereaux siblings.

"Hillary was craving wings. Little Kennedy is teething, and Hillary was up all night, so I thought this would brighten her day."

Paige gave her brother a nudge with her elbow. "You're a good husband and daddy."

"Who would have thought?"

"I knew you had it in you," she said smiling up at her big brother. "You're not staying then? You're taking them home?"

"Yeah. I might have a beer while I wait for my order to finish, though."

At that moment, they called Paige's number. "I'll have one waiting for you at the bar where I'm sitting."

"I'll be right there," Chase said as Paige walked to the truck and picked up her order.

She carried her food inside and set it on the bar. Oliver finished pouring a beer for a patron before moving to stand in front of Paige. He picked up a piece of the cauliflower and dipped it into the ranch before popping it into his mouth.

"These are so good," he said, his mouth full of hot cauliflower.

"Chase is coming in to join me. I told him I'd have a beer ready for him."

Oliver nodded and poured a beer for Chase, setting it next to Paige.

A moment later, Chase sat on the stool next to her and proceeded to take a long sip from his beer. "This is the good one." He looked over at Paige's basket of food. "Those aren't wings."

"Cauliflower."

"Seriously? A wing truck comes to the tap house and you get veggies in sauce."

Paige picked up a piece with her fork and held it out toward her brother. "You should try it. Veggies would do you good."

"I'd rather not," he argued as he lifted his beer to his lips and drank. "What are you doing here anyway? Not watching the football games, surely."

"Maybe," she replied as Oliver walked toward the back room, and she heard her brother laugh.

"There's something going on here," he teased.

"These people are my friends."

"And that one has an eye for you." He nodded in Oliver's direction as he walked from the back room with a box in his hands.

"Hush. You don't know anything."

"I'm not blind, Paige. So what's going on?"

Oliver stopped in front of them, took another bite of the cauliflower, and headed back to the storage room again.

Paige turned in her seat and studied the humored look on her brother's face. "I kissed him."

Chase's brows rose. "You kissed him?"

"Last night after the bar closed, and he drove me to my car. God, I not only kissed him, I pounced on him," she recalled and could feel the heat in her cheeks.

Chase fought the smile that eventually won. "He's a good guy."

"He wants to lend me the money for my studio."

"Everyone wants to do that."

"I might have to take it." Paige pushed her hair from her forehead and tucked it behind her ear. "I don't want anything to be complicated."

Chase finished his beer. "Relationships are complicated. Even marriage is complicated."

"Aren't you happy?"

"Never been happier," he admitted as he set his empty glass on the bar. "Besides, one kiss doesn't constitute a relationship. You've been friends for almost two years now. You hang out, he comes to your classes. Don't you suppose you were acting on impulse after a fun night?"

Was that what she'd done? She wasn't sure. There had been feelings there, hadn't there been? Maybe she did need to think about it a bit more.

Chase finished his beer as the flashing pager from the wing truck lit up next to him signaling that his order was ready. "We all have your back, sis," he said as he set his empty glass on the bar. "So does he."

Standing from the stool, Chase threw down a few dollars for a tip, as the rule was that no Devereaux paid for beer. He kissed Paige on the head and walked out of the tap house to retrieve his dinner and head home.

Paige put her fork into a piece of cauliflower, dipped it into the ranch, and then stared at it for a moment. Contemplating what her brother had said about her and Oliver being friends, she wondered if it would be best to borrow the money from him. After all, if something went south, she lost an acquaintance and didn't put a wall up between herself and a family member. She didn't anticipate losing a friend either, but it would be safer. And maybe, just maybe, Chase was right, and she'd been moved to kiss Oliver last night while riding a Halloween sugared high.

She laughed to herself as she bit the cauliflower off of the fork.

"What's so funny?" Oliver asked.

"Just thinking about something my brother said."

"Where'd he go?"

"His meal was ready and he headed home." She pushed the money toward him and Oliver smiled as he took it and put it into the jar.

"Devereauxs are very generous."

"Devereauxs are appreciative," she countered and took another bite as she contemplated her next lead into their conversation. "I need thirty-four thousand," she said on a quick breath and Oliver lifted his head to look at her.

He moved toward the bar, opposite her, rested his arms on it and took a piece of cauliflower with his fingers and popped it into his mouth.

As he chewed and studied her, her stomach began to tighten. Why had she said that? Seriously what was wrong with her?

"I can have it to you by tomorrow morning."

Was that what she wanted? Had she crossed a line or made a mistake?

Paige bit down on her lip. "Are you sure?"

"I told you I wanted to help you."

"I'm nervous."

"I understand that. I've been in your shoes."

She supposed they all had been. "Thank you."

"I'm excited to see what you do with the place. Can I make one suggestion?"

"Of course."

"Have your brother paint it, and take that old wood paneling off the wall. Seriously, the seventies were almost fifty years ago. We can move on now."

Paige laughed and eased her shoulders. It was going to be okay, she told herself. Oliver was a good friend.

CHAPTER 15

As students arrived bright and early for their morning yoga class, Paige watched the door, waiting for Oliver to walk through, but by the time class started, he hadn't arrived.

He didn't always make it on Monday morning, but then again, he didn't often miss. Maybe she'd spooked him. He'd offered her the money, and maybe now he didn't want to give it to her. Perhaps Oliver didn't even want to see her.

Pushing away the regret, Paige lowered the lights and began class. Deep cleansing breaths in and out, she reminded herself as she said the same to her class. As they moved their bodies, Paige let her mind focus only on the class. Yoga had trained her to clear her mind during practice, and perhaps that's why she'd done it so often.

As they began to move into positions, the door opened and Oliver quietly hurried into the class, unrolled his mat, and began the practice with the other students. Paige kept her gaze soft and focused on the others, afraid to look at Oliver and see his regret.

As the class progressed, Paige walked through the students to help with their positions. A hand on one back, perhaps a gentle adjustment to another's arm. When she moved toward Oliver she noticed how rigid he was and she pressed a hand to his back to help him adjust.

He turned his head and smiled at her, and she looked into a worried set of eyes. Yes, she'd crossed a line. Well, after class, she'd correct that. She didn't want a loan to come between them, especially when he hadn't even given her the money yet.

As the class concluded, Paige guided her students to rest in the corpse pose, their bodies relaxed and their arms to their sides. It was her favorite pose. When she'd started yoga, she'd thought it was a lazy pose, and that was why she enjoyed it so much. But with her longevity in training, she realized it was her favorite because it offered stillness and reflection. She could lay in the pose and collect herself and her thoughts, then walk away from practice fresh and ready to make the most of any day.

"Let your breath push out all of the worry and doubt in your body. Remember your practice today as you go forth. Be mindful of the peace that you feel and bring yourself back to it when you need to gain control again," she said in a calm and soothing tone. "Open your eyes and sit up on your mat. Bring your hands up, taking one last deep breath. Bring them together at your heart. Be grateful as you step out of the door and spread that gratefulness. Namaste," she said, ending the class.

Each student, in their own time, began to rise from their mats and roll them up. Some began conversation immediately, others went on their way silently, only giving acknowledgement with a smile.

When the room was empty, she noticed Oliver still seated on his mat. It wasn't odd for him to be the last one ready to leave. Though now she wondered if it was so he could hang back and talk to her.

Paige rolled up her mat, and as she stood, Oliver opened his eyes to meet hers.

"I'm sorry I was late," he said softly.

"It's okay. This isn't elementary school."

He nodded and moved from his mat, then began to roll it up. "Will you be around later? I was going to bring you that check and obviously, things didn't work out the way I'd planned it."

Paige placed her rolled mat into the basket in the corner of the room. "Maybe we should talk about that," she said as Oliver rose to his feet. "I think it was a mistake. I shouldn't have asked you for—"

"No. It wasn't a mistake," he said, setting his rolled mat on the floor and walking to her. "Things in my life are complicated right now. That doesn't affect me wanting to give you this money."

"I don't want to add to your complications."

He raised his hand to her cheek. "You already have."

Oliver moved in and pressed his lips to hers, lingering there until Paige moved in and wrapped her arms around him.

Deepening the kiss, Oliver slipped his hand around the back of Paige's neck and down her back. She eased against him trying to grasp what was going on. Where were they going with all of this? Were they friends? Did they want to be lovers?

She let the world spin around her as his tongue pressed against hers and she gripped his shirt, hanging on for dear life.

"Oh!" The word echoed through the empty room. "I didn't mean to interrupt," Kennedy said as she turned so that her back was toward them.

Paige let out a breath and Oliver took a moment to assure her with his eyes before kissing her forehead.

"I'd better be going. I'll call you and we can make arrangements."

Paige nodded and watched as he gathered his mat and headed toward the door, stopping briefly to kiss her sister on the cheek before disappearing.

When Kennedy turned, a cup of coffee in each hand, her eyes were wide. "And when did this kick into gear?" she asked as Paige walked toward her taking one of the coffees she offered.

"About right then," she said taking the stopper out of the lid. "Actually, I kissed him on Halloween."

Kennedy lifted her cup to her *Kennedy Pink* painted lips, showing off her freshly painted, matching, manicure. "Do you think this is smart?"

"You're still going on about missing money, and not considering the person behind it," she accused as she walked toward the front of the center and sat in one of the plush chairs by the window.

Kennedy followed. "I like Oliver. I always have. Stuff is happening, and I worry about him. So, I worry about you getting involved."

"I asked him to loan me the money," Paige said quickly before taking a sip of her coffee and watching her sister process the news.

"I'd give you the money."

"So would Chase, Max, and Meghann. So would the bank. I weighed my options and thought if something happened and I lost a friend, it would be easier to deal with than breaking ties with a sibling or an in-law."

"Friend? That didn't look friendly. That looked dangerously hot."

"Stay out of my business," she warned and noticed the pained look in Kennedy's eyes.

"Fine. Be careful with your business and your heart," Kennedy warned. "I came to see what flight you ended up on. I think we're on the same one."

And it was back to practical Kennedy. This, Paige could handle.

CHAPTER 16

As was his ritual, Oliver made himself a power breakfast and headed out to his garage to work out once he returned home from yoga.

Yoga didn't seem to calm him as it had before. He wasn't sure if he should blame that on the card he'd received from his mother, or the fact that being in Paige's presence made him lose focus. He was going to assume it was the latter, because he didn't give a crap that his mother sent him another note.

Oliver cranked up his speaker and Metallica gave a different vibe to the area. He picked up his dumbbells and sat down on his weight bench. Taking a few breaths, he laid back and began his workout, hoping that thinking of the sandman in the lyrics would make everything else in his mind fuzzy.

An hour later, sweaty and slightly less frustrated, Oliver turned off the lights in his garage, and walked through the back door of his house, just as his doorbell rang. He picked up a towel off the dryer, and wiped his face as he walked through the house.

Through the window in the door he could see his business partners standing on his front porch. Suddenly his chest ached. This wasn't a good sign.

Oliver pulled open the door to see the stone faces of the three men looking at him.

"Nice surprise," he said pushing open the screen.

"We needed a business meeting," Jeff said as they all stepped inside.

Oliver watched them all file in, wondering if they were aware of how they huddled together. "I can make us some coffee, or—"

Craig shook his head. "That's okay. Can we just sit and talk?"

A knot began to twist in Oliver's stomach. "Sure. Sit down."

He wished he had a sofa or another chair, but he watched as Jeff sat in one chair and Joel in the other. Craig perched on the arm of one, leaving Oliver to stand and look at his friends.

"So what's so important that you're all here at one time this early in the morning?" he asked folding his arms in front of him.

Joel, who's hands were clasped together, his arms rested on his knees, looked up at him first. "There's more money missing from your shifts," he said.

Oliver bit the inside of his cheek so hard he tasted blood. "That's bullshit."

Jeff shook his head. "The bookkeeper sent us the sheets. What you turn in isn't what they record."

"Then they're wrong," Oliver argued.

Craig stood from the arm of the chair. "Why would they lie to us?"

"Why would I?" He saw that register for his friends, but it didn't bring him any comfort. "If you want to see my books, I'll show you my books. The only deposits are the money the book-keeper sends each of us every week. The money going out is for my bills. Look around. If I'd been stealing from you, wouldn't you think I'd have splurged on nicer furniture?" The volume of his voice grew louder.

Now Joel stood. "You're right, but you also offered to lend Paige the money for her studio."

"Yeah, because, once again, look around. I don't spend a damn cent. I don't believe in material things. I don't need for anything, so I have a nest egg, and I offered to lend it to a friend."

Jeff, still seated, steepled his fingers at his chin. "Would you show us your accounts? I know how shitty it sounds, but it'd relieve some stress on us."

"You guys are unbelievable," Oliver said as he walked to his bedroom and retrieved his laptop from the top of his dresser. As he walked, he opened it and signed into his bank account. "Here. This is what I have. You can see the deposits, and they match your deposits. Yeah, I have a lot in there, once again, because I don't spend anything."

He handed the laptop to Jeff who scrolled through the items and then looked up at the others. "What we pay ourselves is what he has in deposits. Nothing more."

Craig narrowed his eyes. "Well, where is the other account?"

That was the moment Oliver felt the blood fill his cheeks and his fists clenched at his side as he moved toward him, and Joel maneuvered himself between them.

"Whoa!" Joel pushed them apart. "This isn't what we came here to do," he said and Oliver eased back.

"Yeah? I think this is exactly what you came here to do. I'm not stealing from the tap house. I'm not taking more than my fair share. And I'm working my ass off like the rest of you. I put as much money in as each of you did, understanding it was your freaking name that went on the building because it was your plan," he said looking at Jeff and Joel. "What do I gain by stealing from you? I lose you all as my best friends who are like my brothers. I lose my job. I lose my investment. Why would that be worth it to me?"

Joel placed a hand on his shoulder. "We know that's what you'd lose. It just doesn't add up to the numbers. Something's not right, and we need to fix it. We all love you, like you said, like a brother. We don't want any of this to be true."

"It's not true," he reassured them.

"This is what we propose." Joel lowered his hand and took a breath. "For the next two weeks, you don't work the bar. Take some time off. We'll still pay you, you deserve your cut. But then we can see what's happening."

Oliver's hands fisted again as he bit down hard. "I can't believe this."

"I believe you," Joel said. "This is the best way."

"And next week you're going to Hawaii and I was taking some of your shifts. That leaves everything to these two."

"We've discussed it. They'll be fine."

Now he could feel the heat rise in his body. "You're going to find that I haven't touched a damned penny."

"I know that."

"And at what point are you all going to treat me differently? Or am I going to be the bastard you can't trust anymore?"

Joel shook his head. "We don't feel that way."

Oliver shifted a glance in Craig's direction, and was fairly sure that wasn't the case.

"Fine. I'll stay away. You do what you have to do. And you go on your vacation. But when this is over, I expect each of you to apologize to me. You know this is bullshit."

Joel nodded and Jeff stood, handing Oliver back the laptop.

Craig walked out of the house.

Joel ran his hand over the back of his neck. "Sorry this went down like this."

"Isn't it what you expected? You can't show up to someone's house and accuse them and think it's going to end well."

"Right. I know something's up, but I don't think you're involved, for the record."

"It'll mean more when you come back with your apology," he said as he watched the brothers walk out of his house.

CHAPTER 17

Walking toward her car, Paige looked down the street at the tap house. She'd just finished her meeting with Pricilla, the owner of the wellness center, and they'd finalized plans for Paige to purchase the business.

Paige had emptied out her savings to put the deposit down that they'd agreed on, and had signed her intent to purchase. Next week, after she returned from Hawaii, she would meet with Pricilla and her lawyers to finish the transaction.

Though now Paige wondered which of her siblings she was going to ask for the money.

Monday, when Oliver had walked out of her class, it had been the last time she'd spoken to him all week. She understood he was busy, and he too had his own business, but he'd kissed her—oh, had he kissed her—and said he'd call.

Something Paige understood, all too well, was the need to have her space. Surely Oliver was the same. She hadn't called him or sought him out, but now it was Thursday, and she needed to talk to him. If he didn't want to lend her the money, then fine. She'd ask her brother Max for it. He'd sold his business and could afford to lend it to her without consequence. If Oliver was out, then so was she. They'd only shared a few kisses, it wasn't like she'd slept with him or married him. It was innocent. It had been attraction. It was pissing her off and she didn't like it.

Instead of getting into her car, she walked toward the tap house. Joel's truck was parked out back, as well as Jeff's. There was no sign of Oliver's car, or his bicycle for that matter.

Gripping the front of her jacket closed against the cold wind, she opened the door and stepped into the tap house.

"Hey, Paige," Joel greeted her as she walked toward the bar and he stacked glasses on the shelf. "Can I get you something?"

She shook her head. "I was just over at the wellness center and thought I'd come by."

Joel nodded his head slowly and threw the towel he'd picked up over his shoulder. "Everything moving along with the sale?"

"I just met with Pricilla. We'll close when I get back from Hawaii."

"Congratulations." He took the towel and wiped down the bar, then slung it over his shoulder again. "You were able to get your financing then?"

Paige studied him. "I think I have it locked down." She scanned the bar. "Doesn't Oliver work Thursdays?"

Joel took the towel, this time setting it on the bar. "He's taking some time off."

"Time off?"

"He didn't mention it to you?"

Paige crossed her arms in front of her. "Should he? I haven't talk to him since Monday."

Joel reached for a glass and filled it from the water tap. "I think I misunderstood," he said as he sipped from the glass.

"Misunderstood what?"

She could see the color change in his cheeks. "I thought you were seeing each other."

"My sister told you what she saw."

"Of course she did," he offered before he took another sip from the water. "We talk, Paige."

"Well, that's all there was. A few kisses. It's not like I married the guy."

"He's not a bad guy."

Paige was surprised to hear him say that. "I don't think he is. Maybe I'll go find him and see what he's doing with his free time."

As she turned to leave, Joel called out her name and turned to look at him. "Be careful."

She wasn't sure what the hell that was supposed to mean, but she sure didn't like Joel's tone.

OLIVER'S CAR was parked outside of his house and Paige pulled up behind it.

What was she doing? He obviously didn't want to talk to her or anyone else. Why would he be hiding away if that weren't the case?

But Paige never was one to keep her nose out of other's business, at least not when she'd been part of the business to begin with.

As she walked up to the house she could hear Ozzy's voice talking about a crazy train, and the sound of weights being dropped to the ground. It didn't sound as if it were coming from in the house, so she walked through the light dusting of snow on the grass, around the house, and noticed that the lights were on in the garage.

She walked toward the garage when she heard the clanging of weights as if someone were adding more to a bar. The music had changed and now Meatloaf was praying for the end of time.

As Paige reached for the door knob, she stopped and stepped back. If she could hear the music all the way to the street, then he couldn't hear her at all. The last thing she wanted was to walk in on him while he was lifting weights. He'd either drop them on his head or throw them at hers. Neither was an option she wished to be part of.

Instead, she pulled her phone from her coat and texted him.

I'm at your house, outside your garage. Can I come in?

She watched as her message went from delivered to read, and a moment later the door opened and the air turned to steam as it mixed the cold from outside with the warmth he'd created inside.

"I didn't expect to see you here," he said staring at her.

"I didn't know I was coming. But Joel said you were taking some time off, and I wanted to see you. You didn't call on Monday."

Oliver stepped back into the garage and straddled the weight bench. Laying back, he positioned himself under the barbell.

"Do you not talk to your family? I didn't call because I assumed you wouldn't want to hear from me. So imagine my surprise that you're standing here."

Paige now felt the warmth of the room, but she wasn't so sure it wasn't just the heat of her own skin as his words aggravated her.

"What do my family and what's happening between you and me have to do with it?"

He chuckled as he lifted the bar up out of its cradle and onto his chest.

"I'm just surprised you're here, that's all."

She watched as he lifted the bar up and down multiple times, growing slower with each rise until the bar shook and he set it back in the cradle.

"Hop on the treadmill," he said as he sat up and wiped his face. "No need to just watch me do this."

"I don't want to watch at all. I want to talk."

He looked up at her with those dark eyes and studied her. "Back door is open. Make some water for tea and I'll be inside in a few moments."

Paige assumed that was all she'd get, but she'd take it. All she wanted was a few answers. She'd get those and head back home.

CHAPTER 18

Oliver racked his weights and turned off his iPod and speaker. He stood in the silence for a moment contemplating the conversation it appeared he was about to have.

Turning off the light, Oliver walked out of the door, and locked it behind him. The snow had picked up since he'd walked out to the garage, and the chill hit his warm and wet skin.

He could hear the kettle on the stove whirring when he walked through the back door. Paige sat at his small kitchen table, her phone in her hand. There was a comfort in seeing her there that he hadn't expected.

Oliver hung the key to the garage on the hook next to the back door. He kicked off his shoes, reached for a towel off of the dryer, and walked to the kitchen. Wiping the back of his neck with the towel, he watched Paige stand and move to the kettle as it began to whistle. She moved about his tiny kitchen as if she'd been there one hundred times before, pulling down mugs from the cupboard, and carrying over the box of tea as well.

"You know your way around a kitchen," he said as he pulled up a chair and sat down.

"I watched you when I was here last. It wasn't too hard to remember where everything was."

She sat down across from him, and he noted the worry in her eyes. Oliver watched her pour the hot water into the mugs, and he reached for his favorite tea bag. As he tore open the bag, Paige carried the kettle back to the stove, and then joined him back at the table.

"Why didn't you call me on Monday?" she asked as she tore into her tea bag and dunked it into the water.

Oliver took the towel from his neck and threw it into the laundry room behind him, giving himself a moment to think. Blane, who had been resting in his bed, cocked his head to give Oliver a stern look before laying back down. "Like I said. I was sure you'd spoken to your family and didn't want me getting in your business."

"What happened?"

"They didn't fill you in?"

"I want to hear it from you."

Oliver held the end of the tea bag and bobbed it in and out of the water to occupy his mind as it twisted the story with the anger from his heart.

"I came home after leaving the studio, I worked out in the garage, and I came inside just as they all came to the door."

"Who is all?"

"My partners. They came to accuse me of stealing again." He watched her tuck her lips between her teeth as if something might have been said to her. "Anyway, they accused me, I told them I didn't do anything. I showed them my bank account and they wanted to know where I kept my *other* bank account. Paige, I didn't steal anything. The money I have in my account is my share of the company. We each get the same damn thing."

"I've seen you run a drawer. I've never seen you take anything."

"Well, tell that to your brother-in-law."

"How do they know this anyway?" she asked, and he was surprised she was thinking about it any deeper.

"You've seen the process. I close out the drawer. I put the bag in the safe. Every weekday morning, the bookkeeping company comes and takes it. They run the numbers and take the money to the bank."

Paige narrowed her brows. "They take it to the bank?"

"It's a legit company. We've used them for years. But it keeps four sets of hands out of the till."

She shook her head. "It sounds like someone in the company could be messing with it."

"So why just my shift? Why only if my name is on it?" he shook his head as he pulled his tea bag from his mug and sat it on the saucer. "The company is secure. My numbers are right. I think they just want me out."

"No. Joel wouldn't do that to someone. Neither would his brother. If they wanted you out, they'd ask you to leave."

"I've known them a lot longer than your family has. He has a temper. They all do."

"But they have decency too. They wouldn't cheat and lie to get you out of the business."

Oliver pushed away his cup and rested his arms on the table. "You have faith in me?"

"I do."

"You don't really know me."

"I've known you for almost two years. I know enough," she said looking at him with those dark eyes and batting her long lashes.

"Did you come here just for the loan?"

Now she pushed her mug away and stood. Paige walked around the small table and stood in front of him until he turned his body toward her. She took the opportunity to straddle him, wrapping her arms around his neck.

Oliver gripped her hips to hold her in place.

"I came here to see what was going on with a friend. A friend I've grown to care deeply about. I can get the money from anywhere, and I will. I wanted to make sure you were okay."

The sentiment squeezed at his heart. "You care deeply about me?"

"I do."

"Not to make it sound strange, but my grandparents were the only other people to ever tell me they cared deeply about me."

"You're worth caring about."

Now he could feel the tremble begin in his fingers and work its way through his limbs. Paige Devereaux cared for him even when the world had turned against him.

He lifted his hand to her cheek and she covered it with her hand.

"Paige, getting involved with me is going to be a mistake for you. Nothing ever goes right for me, as you can see."

"I don't believe that."

"You should."

She lowered her face until it was only a breath away from his. "I'll make my own judgements on that," she said before she leaned in and kissed him, her mouth taking full possession of his, forcing him to pull her even closer.

When they stopped long enough for a breath, he looked into her eyes and saw a lust, a passion, a caring sprit. He could easily fall in love with this woman and it was completely the wrong time to do so.

"I should go get a shower," he said. "Maybe we can go get some lunch, or dinner."

Paige rose and took his hand. "I'll scrub your back," she said as she pulled him up from his chair and toward the bathroom where, once inside, she kicked the door closed behind her.

CHAPTER 19

Paige wasn't sure how clean Oliver had gotten in the shower. Whatever had come over her had caused her to nearly attack the man, whose bed she now laid in, wrapped in his arms.

But she'd made the move because her heart and her body felt the need for it, and she was grateful.

Under the warm stream of water, under the lather they had soaped up on one another's body, she studied the tattoos he hid from his grandmother on his back, his chest, his arm, and the one on his hip. And Oliver had massaged every knot out of her neck as she was pressed up against the cold tile.

They'd explored and kissed, and moved their friendly relationship into something much more serious until the water ran cool, then they moved to the bedroom.

When her stomach grumbled, she realized they'd never gotten lunch, or dinner. They'd spent the day wrapped in his sheets, and one another's arms.

The moment was interrupted when the alarm on her cell phone chimed and she reached over Oliver's body to silence it.

"Do you have a date?" he asked, his voice soft and full of sleep and Paige watched as the cat wandered into the room, looked around, and headed back out.

"I have my late class. I need to get to the school."

Oliver let out a small moan. "I forgot about your class."

"I almost did too."

Paige rolled out of the bed fully aware that Oliver watched as she hurried to the bathroom to collect her clothes from where she'd discarded them. She carried them back to the bedroom.

"Will I see you in class tomorrow morning?" she asked in a whisper, which was unnecessary, but felt right.

"Won't I see you later?"

Paige slipped her legs into her pants and tugged them up. "You want me to come back?"

"Or I could go to your house, unless this was just a day of fun, and doesn't mean anything at all."

Paige moved to the bed and sat down next to him, sans her top and only her jeans on. "I don't think that at all. I don't sleep with men for fun. I mean just for fun. I mean..."

"I know what you mean. We can take it slower," he teased. "Or I could come to class with you now."

"You've never been to one of my late classes."

"I'll get dressed."

As she watched him rise and pull clothes from his drawers, she finished dressing, and tried to control the shaking that had begun in her body.

Had she jumped into bed too quickly with him? She was the suggestive one, but she'd wanted it. No, this was right. She did like him, and she had since she'd met him. They'd been friends for two years now. Even if this ended up being a quick roll in bed and nothing else happened, their friendship could survive it. Lots of people had friends with benefits.

She laughed to herself as she pulled on her shirt. He was a chiseled Adonis. She figured she'd hit the jackpot in the sex department, no matter what happened in the friend or lover department.

OLIVER WONDERED how people made it to eight o'clock yoga classes. Usually he was working, and he didn't get off work until the wee hours of the morning. But since he'd had a lazy day in the arms of the sexy yoga instructor, he found that as they finished their practice, he couldn't stop yawning.

There was some relief when she said, "Namaste," and ended class. He was sure he'd fall asleep if they sat still much longer.

As the class cleared out and headed home in the snow, Oliver rolled up his mat.

"I was surprised that many people showed. Usually if it's snowing, I have fewer students," Paige said as she turned off the music and rolled up her mat.

"That's good for the bottom line. It means they appreciate what you offer and they don't want to miss a single class."

"You're right."

As she walked past him, he caught her arm and pulled her to him. "Let me loan you the money."

"Oliver, you have a lot on your plate right now. Why don't we just let this go? I'll find the money and—"

"I want to do this. I want to see you succeed in what you love. I don't know what will happen to me and my business, but I have a chance to help you start something amazing."

Paige wrapped her arms around his neck. "You're sure?"

"Absolutely."

She pressed her forehead against his. "And what if this doesn't work out between us? It's new, and—"

"It's been building for two years. Maybe we should look at it as if we almost missed our opportunity and we've taken it extremely slow."

Paige laughed. "You're right. We took it very slow."

Oliver ran his hand over her hair. "Will you come home with me again? Stay with me tonight?"

"You're sure?"

"I wouldn't have asked otherwise. If I'm misreading this, you have to let me know. But I think we're starting something serious here, something longer than just one night?"

Paige drew in a breath. That was what she wanted. "Yes. I'm not one to just jump into bed with someone. If I do, it means something."

"Good. Then I think we're on the same page," he said lowering his mouth to hers and pressing a kiss to her lips. "Let's go home, make some dinner, and discuss business. Then maybe we can seal the deal all night long."

Paige rested her head on his shoulder. After watching her brothers and sister fall in love over the past two years, she hadn't realized just how much she'd longed for the same thing. Was this it? Was Oliver her one and only? He'd warned her that things wouldn't go smoothly, and she didn't care. She believed in his innocence when it came to the money at the tap house too.

As she eased back and looked up into his eyes, she felt the tug in her heart. They'd been friends for years, but her heart was tumbling right into love with the man.

CHAPTER 20

I t had been years since Paige had given up sleep to be with a man. As she closed up the studio after her Friday morning class, she felt the drain of energy that was going to require a strong cup of coffee.

She'd promised her sister that she would help her put up the Christmas decorations at her store. Kennedy thought that since they'd be gone a week in November, it would be best to get the store decorated a few weeks earlier than she normally would have.

Kennedy had arranged for her former employee Clare to run the store while they were all in Hawaii, so she would be there too, becoming acquainted with any new merchandise and systems.

Paige hurried down the street from the wellness center to her sister's store, her coat open and the air nipping at her skin. She pushed open the pink doors and the bells above the door chimed to announce her.

"Paige?" her sister's voice came from the back room.

"Yeah."

"We're all back here."

Paige pulled off her coat and draped it over her arm. She

BERNADETTE MARIE

looked around the store filled with feminine designs and colors. Her sister knew what she'd wanted to build, and she'd done an amazing job. Hopefully, soon, her sister would walk into her yoga studio and think the same of Paige.

When she walked into the back room her sister-in-law Hillary, and her sister Kennedy sat at the table each with a cup of coffee in front of them.

"The pot of coffee is fresh," her sister said. "Help yourself. You look like you need it."

Paige hung her coat on the hook by the back door, pulled down a mug, and filled it. Kennedy had already seen how tired she was, surely this conversation would start going in that direction.

"How many trees are we putting up today?" Paige asked, leaning up against the counter.

"Four. I bought a new pink, flocked one last year, and I can't wait to see it go up. It'll go up in the window with glittery pink baubles."

Paige smiled when she watched her sister's eyes light up. "Alright. I'm ready."

Hillary shook her head. "We're not. Teething children at our houses. We need a few moments to get our energy back."

Paige walked to the open chair and sat down. She'd rather just set up trees, but it looked as if she was going to get her fill of sisterly gossip.

Kennedy lifted her mug to her lips. "Did you have a full class today?"

"I did," Paige admitted. "I might have to open up one more morning."

"That's good."

"Very good."

"And why are you so tired today?" Kennedy asked peering over the top of her mug.

"I'm just fine, sis."

"You just look tired is all."

How much was Paige willing to tell them? Kennedy would surely be on the side of her husband when it came to thinking that Oliver was stealing from their company. But Paige wanted her to be happy for her, so perhaps now wasn't the time to gossip about her love life.

"I had a lot on my mind last night. That's all."

Somehow that managed to divert the conversation to shipments that were going to be arriving and plans to get to the airport in one of Chase's cars with one of his other drivers.

When Clare arrived, there was no more attention paid to how tired Paige was or the fact that within a week they'd be in Hawaii. It was time to transform the store.

OLIVER HAD MOPPED HIS FLOORS, washed the few dishes in his sink, and cleaned the bathroom. It seemed as if having time on his hands was foreign to him. For years he'd get up in the morning and head out to the tap house they were working on and create. Once in a while, he'd find himself working on one of the rentals that the Kingsley brothers owned as well.

He loved his work, and not being part of it was killing him.

As he tidied up the living room, he noticed the birthday cards still on the table that he'd received nearly a week earlier. Warmth filled him when he looked at his grandmother's card.

Then he picked up the dinosaur card. When he'd seen his mother's name on it, he hadn't even read what she'd written inside. He hadn't cared.

Now it seemed necessary to look at it.

Sitting down in the chair he opened the card and looked at the handwriting. It wasn't even familiar to him, but he could have picked his grandmother's out from a hundred samples if asked to.

· · ·

DEAREST OLIVER,

Happy birthday. I've lost count. How many will this be? I've been keeping tabs on you, and I want you to know how proud I am of you. I saw the write up in a local paper about the tap house you and your friends built. It must be going well.

I sent you a letter a few weeks ago, but I haven't heard from you. Times are hard, Oliver. I haven't been in touch with your father for almost eighteen years, and my health isn't the best.

I'm not asking anything from you, like I said, I keep an eye on what you're doing. And you're doing well. Maybe someday you'll want to see me. I'd like to see you.

Love, Mom

OLIVER GRIPPED the card hard enough that it folded under the pressure. His own mother didn't even know how old he was. And where had his father gone? He'd never reached out to Oliver after his grandparents had taken him to live with them.

He looked at the card again. His mother had been watching him. Had she been to the tap house? Would Oliver know her if he saw her?

And what was that about her health? Was she looking for sympathy or help? Did he owe that to her? Did he care?

Oliver leaned his head back against the chair. Of course he cared. What kind of son would he be if he didn't care that his own mother was sick? But he didn't owe her anything. Nothing.

The 'free' lifestyle they had lived until he was eight had put him behind in school. His health had been at risk, and his safety had always been in jeopardy.

So much of his time living with his parents was now a blur. His grandparents had given him a life. His grandmother tutored him until he was above grade level, and his grandfather took him fishing and taught him how to play basketball. When he was a varsity athlete, that was because of the love and discipline he had at home with his grandparents.

Oliver stood and took the card to the kitchen. He tore it in half and deposited it into the trash can under the sink.

He didn't need to think of his past. Right now, in the present, he had enough problems—but he also had Paige.

CHAPTER 21

Three out of the four Christmas trees had been put up, and Paige wasn't sure how it was possible, but the store was more pink than when she'd walked in.

She'd never shared her sister's feminine flair, but she enjoyed watching Kennedy bask in it.

As Paige and Hillary sat on the floor near the front window assembling the new tree, she heard the back door open and Joel's voice resonated in her ears. He'd gotten Kennedy's attention and the two had disappeared into Kennedy's office.

There was an unease that had come with seeing him walk in the way he had.

Just as she and Hillary finished assembling the tree, Joel stormed out of the office and through the back door. She'd never seen them fight. What on earth could have happened to have caused that?

When Kennedy emerged, she didn't look distraught as if her husband had taken in after her. There was a sense of worry, but not anguish.

Hillary was the first to ask if everything was okay, and for that Paige was grateful.

Kennedy walked toward them, picking up a box of ornaments as she crossed the room. Clare left her post at the other tree and joined them.

"They're missing more than they thought," she said softly as if to keep it secret between them. "It's been steadily disappearing and they can't find it."

Hillary took the box of ornaments from Kennedy. "They thought it was Oliver."

Paige felt the tightening in her chest, and worked to force her face from showing her discomfort with the conversation.

"They did. It was consistently on his shift. So, at the beginning of the week they asked him to take some time off while they sorted it out."

Hillary turned to Paige. "You've been spending time with him. What's going on?" she asked as if Paige would have a simple answer.

"I don't know. I think someone is stealing from the company, but I don't think it's Oliver. In fact, with all my heart I believe that."

Kennedy crossed her arms in front of her. "Is it your heart that makes you say that?"

Paige and Kennedy had never had one of those sister relationships where words and claws came to play. Kennedy was older and had been like a second mother to Paige when her own mother died. They'd had a respect for each other as women, but now Paige felt attacked.

"Matters of my heart are none of your business."

"You're seeing a man who is stealing from my family."

Paige's breath caught in her lungs and Hillary stepped between them. "Ken, that's a mighty big statement there."

Kennedy batted her eyes against tears that had begun to pool. "It all leads to Oliver. How can you stand there and defend him over my husband?"

Paige pursed her lips. "Because I believe he's innocent."

"Why? What makes you think that?"

"Have you been to his house? He doesn't even own furniture. Why in the hell would someone who doesn't need things need to steal money? He's paid the same as the other four. He's doing okay for himself."

Kennedy's shoulders hunched. "Then where is the money going?"

"How in the hell am I supposed to know?" Paige argued. "There are four partners and a slew of employees. Not to mention the bookkeeping service. So don't point your finger at one man. What if it's your husband?"

Kennedy's eyes went wide before the tears streamed down her cheeks. "Joel would never do that."

"Neither would Oliver."

Wiping at her eyes, Kennedy took a step back. "You're in love with him, aren't you?"

"I didn't say that."

"You're willing to fight for him over family. The only reason you would do that was if you were in love with him."

Paige fisted her hands and released them. "I think he's innocent. I don't have to be in love with him to think that."

Hillary and Clare shifted their heads almost as if they were watching a tennis match, and now it was Kennedy's turn to hit the ball.

"I saw how you were with him. You don't kiss someone like that if you're not in love."

Paige bit down on her lip. "Sure you do. It's just attraction. It's just sex, and it's way off topic. What I think you need to do is tell your husband to keep digging and not assume someone is guilty until all the proof has been collected."

Hillary stepped between them again facing Paige. "You're sleeping with Oliver?"

"Who is Oliver?" Clare asked trying to keep up with the conversation.

Hillary looked at her. "Joel's business partner."

"Oh, this gets deep fast," Clare said looking back toward Paige.

"Again, my sex life isn't the topic here and I think it's time for me to go home."

Paige pushed through her friends and past her sister on her way to the back room to collect her coat from the hook. Instead of going out the front door, she walked out the back and down the narrow alley until she came to the end of the building where the wellness center was located, and her car was parked in the lot.

Pulling her key fob from the pocket of her coat, she hit the unlock button over and over until she reached the car and pulled open the door. Sliding inside, she gripped the cold steering wheel and pressed her forehead to it, her breath carrying on the air.

She was torn between her loyalty and love for her sister, and her feelings for the man she was sure she was falling in love with. But hadn't she followed through on her feelings for Oliver knowing that she was willing to let him go if things went badly and it would save her relationship with her family?

So why was it she wasn't feeling that way at that moment?

There was no doubt in Paige's mind that Oliver wasn't stealing the money, but she too had no proof in that. Next week she'd be in Hawaii with her family, and she'd have no choice but to mend her relationship with her sister. But until then, she wanted to be with Oliver.

CHAPTER 22

I'm cooking. Join me? Stay the night? The text interrupted Paige's pity party in her car.

She let out a breath that carried on the cool air. It was exactly what she wanted. *I'll be there,* she replied.

Paige started her car, and as it warmed, she took the hair tie on her gearshift and tied up her hair. As soon as the heater had taken the chill out of the car, Paige drove toward her house.

She'd collected the mail from the box and packed a bag to stay at Oliver's overnight. Before she headed out, she checked her email. Her father had sent out the itinerary for the week in Hawaii. There were times and dates for dinners, photos, and the wedding. He and Gloria had planned a private luau and a reception dinner after the wedding.

Paige pressed her fingers to her temples and rubbed away the headache that was forming. Who looked at an itinerary for a vacation in Hawaii and dreaded it?

Before she depressed herself further, she picked up the bag she'd packed and drove to Oliver's.

. . .

As Paige stood on Oliver's front porch, the lights from inside welcoming her with warmth. She felt the tension that had been tight in her shoulders begin to release as she rang the doorbell.

Oliver smiled as he pulled open the door. Paige took in the sight of him barefoot in his jeans, with the button unfastened. She could see the tattoo on his chest through the thin fabric of his T-shirt. There was no product in his hair so it flopped to the side and brushed his brows. He was completely relaxed and at peace in his own space.

"Something smells good," she said as he stepped back for her to pass by him.

"Zucchini noodles in a garlic sauce."

Paige set her bag on the floor near the wall and shrugged out of her coat. Just as she did, Oliver took it from her and hung it on the rack behind him. Then he moved to her, dipping his head to press kisses to her neck.

"You're in a good mood," she managed to say as her eyes closed and her body began to tingle.

"I'm happy to see you. I can't remember when I've spent so much time all alone."

His words crushed her. He shouldn't be alone. Oliver should be a the tap house working his shifts.

Paige eased back. "You're doing okay though, right?"

Oliver lifted a hand to her cheek and brushed his thumb over her skin. "I'm doing fine. They're going to find out what's going on, and they're going to find out it's not me. All three of those men are decent men, and they'll come apologizing. I just have to be patient."

"I don't think I could be that calm if I felt attacked."

Oliver shrugged as he gathered Paige in his arms. "I don't have a choice. I can be mad and dive into a deep depression, or I can honor myself by knowing I did nothing wrong, and my friends will soon find that out."

She wasn't so sure about that. Hadn't she walked out on her

sister over them finding more money missing and blaming it on Oliver?

There wasn't much time to worry over it as Oliver moved his mouth to hover over hers. "I'm glad you're here," he said again before kissing her and wiping her mind completely clear of the thoughts that were causing her anxiety.

As he eased back, Paige wiggled her nose when his beard tickled it. "You have a way of making me forget things on the outside of this house."

Oliver nipped her lips with his one more time. "Good. We could both use a little time to unwind." He took her hand and began to lead her to the kitchen. "Let's eat this and then we can relax the rest of the night."

It was hard for Oliver to keep his eyes off of Paige while she ate dinner, and even harder to just stay in his seat and not touch her. His grandmother had always told him that when he needed someone, or something, it would come to him. Was Paige the someone he needed in this desperate time?

"What did you think?" he asked as she took the last bite.

"This was amazing," she said as she wiped her mouth with the napkin. "When I make zoodles, they don't compare."

"My grandmother took the time to teach me how to cook. Though she's a meat and potato kind of gal, and brownies for dessert, kind of woman. But she thought if I was only going to eat vegetables, then I should know how to make them taste good."

"She sounds incredible."

Oliver eased back in his chair and crossed one leg over the other. "I'm glad you said that. I want you to meet her."

"I'd love to meet her."

"Good. She's cooking dinner for my birthday on Sunday, and I'd like you to go with me."

Paige picked up her glass of wine and watched him over the top of it as she sipped. "Your birthday is on Sunday?"

"Yes."

"And this is the first you're mentioning of it?"

"I don't celebrate birthdays like many people do. My grandma makes me dinner, and that's the celebration."

"Birthdays are big deals."

"Not when you don't even know if it's really your birthday." He uncrossed his legs and leaned his arms on the table. "I was born in that park in a teepee. There were no records kept. My mother thinks that November ninth is my birthday, so when my grandmother took custody of me, she got me a birth certificate and that's what she put on it. She sends me a card a week earlier, and it covers all bases."

Paige reached for his hand and interlocked their fingers. "You are a unique man, Oliver Westcott."

"We're all unique. So will you go with me?"

"I'd be honored."

His smile widened as he looked at her.

When they'd started the renovation on the tap house and they'd met the women next door, Oliver had never imagined that he'd be right where he was. He'd initially thought Kennedy was stuck up, but he'd learned that she was a fine business woman, and Joel had swept her off her feet. For a brief moment Hillary had caught his eye, but once he'd met Paige, he knew she was someone special.

He couldn't have pictured where they were right at that moment. A friendship had blossomed, and he'd always been grateful for that. But as she brushed her thumb over his knuckles, he could see a life with her.

When she stood, still holding his hand, and settled in his lap, he was certain of it. When her lips came to his, he knew his heart had tumbled where it had never gone before.

CHAPTER 23

Blane kneaded his paws on Oliver's chest, and it stirred him awake. He noticed Paige in the corner of the room pulling on clothes, and he lifted on his elbows to watch.

"Where are you going?" he asked softly.

She turned to him, her hair spilling over her shoulders, and smiled. "I have a class."

"Right."

She skirted the bed and walked toward him, pressing a kiss to his lips. "Why don't you come over to my house tonight?"

"I'll need directions."

She laughed. "I'll text them to you. I'll see you later."

A moment later she walked out of the room, and he closed his eyes when he'd heard the front door close.

Blane circled the bed and came back to him to nuzzle up against him and rest in the crook of his arm.

"I think I love her," he said to the cat that was obviously not interested. "She'll choose her family over me though, if I don't get this money thing sorted out."

They'd asked him to take time away, and he was doing that. They'd struggle slightly when Joel went to Hawaii, and there'd be no Devereauxs in town to help out in a pinch. Oliver had nothing to hide, so he wasn't going to crawl back or be fearful. They'd see that a mistake had been made. They'd see that he was as honest as the rest of them.

His thoughts were disturbed when his cell phone buzzed on the dresser. Pushing Blane off of his arm, he kicked his legs over the edge of the bed, stood, and retrieved the phone as it buzzed in his hand again.

Not sure why it humored him when his grandmother texted him, he laughed as he picked up a pair of pants and slid them on.

His grandmother didn't much care for technology, and when he'd bought her a smart phone she'd scoffed at it. But, when she found out she could play Candy Crush for hours, she suddenly didn't think it was too bad. Still, she'd usually call before she'd text.

He unlocked his phone and clicked on the text message.

She's here.

Oliver checked the contact information, and it was his grand-mother's, but the message was cryptic.

Who? he replied.

A few minutes later, after he'd started the kettle on the stove, his phone chimed again. He unlocked the screen and read his grandmother's text.

Your mother.

Oliver read the text over and over again before forcing himself to sit down in a chair. After all these years, she was suddenly persistent in getting his attention. Well, now she had it.

He knew his grandmother would never turn away her child, but he also knew she feared her too.

Taking the kettle off of the stove, he hurried to his room to get dressed. He wasn't going to let his grandmother face his mother alone.

❧

OLIVER PULLED up in front of his grandmother's house, and immediately noticed the BMW with temporary plates on it. Surely that was a neighbor's car. He stepped out of his car and nearly sprinted to the door, pulling open the screen and pushing in the front door as if his grandmother had texted saying she was in distress.

The moment he stepped into the house he could feel the tension.

His grandmother sat on the sofa, her hands neatly folded in her lap over the apron she wore. In the other chair, across the room, sat a woman he didn't even recognize.

As he stepped into the room, his mother rose from her chair. "Oliver?"

Oliver shifted a glance toward his grandmother as if for approval to speak to the woman. His grandmother's eyes were damp.

He studied the woman across from him, who looked as if she might have been shopping at Kennedy's store with her exquisite outfit, perfectly styled hair, and a diamond ring on her finger. If this was indeed his mother, the last time he'd seen her, her blonde hair hung to her waist, and she might have weighed all of one hundred pounds. She was sprawled out on the ground, passed out by something she'd taken. Things had changed for Daisy Westcott over the years.

Daisy lifted her hands to her mouth. "I don't know what I expected. I know you're thirty, but I think I expected a little boy to walk through the door."

He supposed they were both stunned then.

Daisy held out her hand. "Oliver."

There was no draw, no need to go to her.

She retracted her hand. "I understand. You haven't responded to my letter or my card. I didn't know how else to reach you, except to come here."

"Now you're here. What do you want?"

Daisy's eyes widened as if the anger in his voice surprised her. "I wanted to see you. It's your birthday."

"Tomorrow is my birthday."

His mother shifted a glance toward his grandmother, whose eyes were on him.

"Right. After all these years, I just really wanted to see that you're doing well."

"I'm doing just fine."

"You look good. I can't believe you have a beard and tattoos," she said smiling, and he realized he hadn't even considered what he was wearing. When his grandmother had texted him, he'd thrown on the shirt he'd worn the day before and had run out of the house. He hadn't even taken a coat.

"Now you've seen me. What else can we do for you?"

Again, he watched Daisy's face shift from a smile to surprise that he'd dismiss her, but he was.

"I'd love to take you to dinner for your birthday."

"I have plans for my birthday."

He'd seen his grandmother's lips tremble into a small smile.

"Okay. Well, I suppose I should go then."

Daisy picked up her coat from the chair and pulled it on. Surely she'd been shopping at Kennedy's, as the coat looked just like the one in the window last month. Then she picked up her purse, a nice leather one, and hung it on her shoulder.

"It was nice to see you again, Mom," she said, and Oliver watched his grandmother only nod. "And, Oliver, you have turned into a handsome man. I'm glad you're so successful in your business."

As she started past he reached for her arm. "What do you know of my business?"

"It's not hard to find people nowadays on social media. I've seen what you and your friends have built. I've been there a few times. Not when you were there, but..."

"Don't go back," Oliver said as he let go of her arm and waited for her to walk out.

Daisy shifted a look between both of them before letting herself out.

Oliver moved to the window and watched as she walked toward the new BMW and then drove away in it.

"I was hoping that was a neighbor's car," he scowled.

"She seems to be doing okay now."

"Good. Then she won't need us," he said turning to see his grandmother still seated with her hands folded in her lap. Her eyes had a light to them now, as if his mother leaving had lifted a burden.

"Let's discuss those tattoos," she said, her brows lifted as she pursed her lips.

So much for hiding them, he thought as he reached for his grandmother's hand and helped her to her feet.

CHAPTER 24

P aige locked the door to the wellness center after class and looked down the street. The lights were on in Kennedy's store, and she knew that her sister would be there.

It would be easy to walk away, drive home, and no one would think a thing about it. But she and Kennedy were tighter than that. She needed to go to the store and smooth things over with her sister.

Pulling up her hood to keep the snow from her eyes, she walked toward her sister's store. Kennedy had a customer, and Paige knew that it would be the perfect time to walk in. Kennedy would remain professional until the customer left.

When the chimes over the door rang, Kennedy lifted her head to greet the person walking in. Paige saw the strain in the smile, but Kennedy kept it in place.

"Hey, Paige."

"Hey. Can I grab a cup of coffee?"

"Of course," she said dripping in sweetness, but Paige heard the bite in it.

Paige walked to the back room, shrugging off her coat, and

draping it over the back of the chair. She moved to the cupboard and pulled down a mug as she looked out the window that faced the back door of the tap house. Craig was working the shift that Oliver would normally cover, and it twisted Paige up inside to think they'd dismissed him. But Oliver was bigger than petty accusations, so she could be too.

Paige opened the door to the refrigerator and pulled out the creamer she knew her sister hid behind the bottles of water she kept for clients. Paige poured it into the coffee and replaced it right where Kennedy kept it.

She sat alone, drinking her coffee, for a while, and then she heard the sound of the chimes above the door and knew that the customer had left. A moment later Kennedy walked through the doorway.

"I'm surprised to see you today. I figured I wouldn't see you until you got on that plane Wednesday morning," Kennedy said as she pulled a mug from the cupboard and poured coffee into it.

"I contemplated that. But you and I aren't like that. I'm not going to let a difference of opinion pull my sister and I apart."

Kennedy leaned her hip against the counter. "I'm glad. I'm sorry I got so heated yesterday. Joel is really upset, and well..."

"He should be upset. I don't blame either of you for that."

Kennedy moved to the table and pulled out the chair. As she sat she set her mug on the table. "You're okay though?"

Paige narrowed her gaze on her sister. "Of course I'm okay."

"I mean, I know you and Oliver are, well..."

"We're seeing each other."

"Right. I just don't want you to get hurt."

"I'm not going to get hurt."

Kennedy wrapped her hands around the mug. "Some woman has been coming to the tap house looking for him. I think she came to the store, too."

Paige felt her mouth go dry. She picked up the coffee mug and drank down what was left. "Okay. So?"

"I'm just saying it's odd. All of this happening and then some woman comes looking for him? I don't know what he's into."

Paige wasn't going to fight her sister, not today. "He's not into anything. He's laying low because his friends asked him to. And as for me, I'm really enjoying his company, Ken. I mean really enjoying it."

She watched Kennedy cringe at the conversation, but she understood.

"Okay. Use your head over your heart. I have to say that. What kind of sister would I be if I didn't?"

"I love you. It's all going to be okay. You'll see." Paige stood and washed her mug. "I'll see you bright and early on Wednesday morning."

"I'll see you then," Kennedy said as Paige kissed her on the top of the head before swinging on her coat and heading out of the store.

Paige hurried to her car to fight off the chill, but she also wanted to get back home as soon as she could. Her sister had gotten into her head, and now she was doubting things. Why would a woman be looking for Oliver? She hated that she was going to do it, but she needed a quick internet search on the man she was sleeping with.

AN HOUR LATER, Paige was satisfied that Oliver Westcott was nothing but a decent man. She'd found him on Facebook and Instagram, where he mostly had photos of his cat, the tap house progress when they'd been renovating it, and the happenings at the tap house since. She did find humor in the fact that he also kept an ongoing photo documentation of his beard length.

When she googled his name, nothing came up out of the ordinary. By all accounts, he was who he said he was, and Paige was satisfied with that.

When her phone buzzed, it startled her. She looked down and smiled at the text on the screen.

Were you going to let me know where you live?

Paige laughed to herself. She had told him she'd send him her address. It had been a hot minute since she'd brought a man home, but she knew she wanted Oliver there.

She texted him the address and he confirmed that he'd be there by five. Paige decided she'd better figure out what to make for dinner. They could go out, but considering the current state of things at the tap house, she just didn't feel like going out in public.

One more search on Pinterest and she found a meal that would be easy to shop for and easy to make. With that, she wrote out a shopping list and headed to the store. Perhaps while she was out she could find something for Oliver's birthday. It surely wouldn't have too much sentiment, but she assumed he'd understand since he hadn't made a big deal out of the date anyway.

Another thought crossed her mind, and she added a stop to Gladys' flower shop to her list as well. She wasn't going to go to his grandmother's house the next day empty-handed, that was for sure.

CHAPTER 25

W hen Paige opened the door to Oliver, he swept in and gathered her in his arms. His mouth came to hers, hot and heavy. She wrapped her arms around his neck as he hoisted her to his hips and against the wall nearest the door.

It had been unexpected, a bit wild, and more than sexy, she thought, as he skimmed his lips down her neck and his beard grazed her skin.

He moved back to her lips, her back still pressed against the wall. Oliver took what she had to offer. Then he carried her to the sofa where he laid her down beneath him and began to undress her.

They moved about in the confined space, lips never parting, until skin pressed to skin. Whatever his need, his urgency, she met him. Teeth skimmed skin as the pace quickened, and then the inevitable happened—they fell off the sofa and to the floor.

Paige's head bounced off the hardwood, and she lifted her hand to soothe it.

"Oh, shit! Paige, I'm so sorry," Oliver rose on up above her and looked down at her with eyes filled with concern. "Are you hurt? Did I hurt you? God, tell me you're okay."

"I'm okay," she said reaching her other hand to his heaving chest. "That was a bit ambitious."

"I should have taken my time," he said, straddling her on his knees and raking his fingers through his hair. "You probably think I'm a monster."

Paige cupped her hand around the back of his neck and pulled him down to her. "I don't think you're a monster. I think you're attracted to me, and I sure as hell know I'm attracted to you."

"Yeah, I am."

"So this was exciting," she said giving his beard a tug. "Maybe we should finish this right here on the floor. No one will get hurt."

Oliver lowered his mouth to hers. "I like your thinking, Devereaux."

MUCH LATER, they sat at the kitchen table. Paige with only a large T-shirt and her panties on, and Oliver in only his jeans. They hadn't taken their eyes off one another since the moment he'd walked in the door.

"My grandmother saw my tattoos," he admitted as he bit into a brussels sprout.

"And how did that go down?" Paige asked.

"Better than I'd thought, but my mother had her rattled, so what was a tattoo or three on her grandson?"

Paige bit the sprout off the end of her fork and studied him. "Your mother?"

"Yeah, it appears that me refusing to contact her after she wrote to me caused her to look me up and come find me. My grandmother texted me this morning that my mother was at her house, so I ran over as fast as I could."

Paige chewed the sprout and then took a sip of her water. "What happened?"

Oliver eased back in his chair and took comfort in Paige's questions. He'd never discussed his mother with anyone before, and he appreciated that he wanted to be open and discuss the situation with her.

"Not a lot really, but I wasn't very gracious." He picked up his water and sipped. "I wouldn't have recognized her if I'd seen her on the street. The last time I'd seen her she was passed out on the floor of the teepee. Today she was driving a new BMW and looked like she'd walked out of Kennedy's store."

Paige's head lifted when he'd said that. "Kennedy said a woman had been at the tap house a few times asking about you, and that she'd been to her store."

"Well, there you go. She's been poking around for a while. Lovely."

"Don't you want to talk to her? I mean, it sounds like she got her life together."

Oliver shook his head. "It looked like she got her life together. That can be bought, though I can't imagine she could handle money well. She did have a diamond on her finger though, that was intriguing and not something we discussed."

"What about your father?"

"In the birthday card she'd sent, she said she hadn't seen him in eighteen years."

Paige reached her hand out to cover his. "Are you okay with all of this?"

"The timing sucks. I'd like to deal with only one problem at a time, but it's my style to pile them on. I told you, things don't usually go my way."

"Some things do," she said, smiling at him across the table.

Oliver stood, taking her hand which covered his, and eased her out of her seat. "You're right. I think this is going in the right direction."

"I think so too," Paige agreed as she eased against him, and wrapped her arms around his neck.

"Next week when I write you that big check, we'll see if you still like me."

Paige eased back. "You don't have to do that. I can get the money."

Oliver rested his hand on her cheek. "I want to. Seriously, I want to be part of what you're creating. It's going to be epic."

"You're sure?"

Oliver let his hands slide down over her bottom and gather her even closer. "I've never been more sure about anything. Take my money, Paige."

Paige cupped Oliver's face in her hands. "Thank you. You won't regret it. I promise."

CHAPTER 26

Paige rolled over and draped her arm over Oliver's chest. "Happy birthday, handsome." She pressed a kiss to his neck and he moaned as he pulled her closer.

"This already is the best birthday I've ever had."

"I doubt that," she teased, and he pulled her on top of him.

"I'm serious. Birthdays come and go. If I'm really lucky, I get a spaghetti dinner with my grandmother, but that's usually it."

Paige rested her chin on his chest. "You deserve more."

"Never needed more."

Paige shifted to pull open the drawer on the nightstand and took out a small box. "I got you a little something. It's nothing much, but..."

"Paige, you didn't have to do that."

"I wanted to." She rolled so that she was next to him, propped up on her elbow, she watched him untie the bow and pull the lid from the box. "It's not much. I didn't know it was your birthday, or I could have put more thought into it."

Oliver lifted the pocket watch from the box, and held it in front of him. "Oh, wow, Paige. This is amazing."

"I saw it in the window of one of the antique shops when I

went to get flowers for your grandmother for today. It reminded me of you," she said. "You know, with your old time beard and all." She reached up and gave it a tug which caused him to laugh.

"I do have mustache wax," he teased and Paige wrinkled her nose.

"I think that might be a bit too old time."

Oliver examined the watch. "My grandfather had a watch like this when I was little. I know he pawned it to buy me a bicycle. They hadn't planned to be raising a kid in their sixties." He turned to look at her. "You don't know what this means to me."

But she saw it in his eyes, and it made her insides turn mushy. "Happy Birthday."

As PAIGE STEPPED out of the car, she felt her insides tighten. She couldn't remember the last time she'd been in a relationship where she went to meet the man's grandparents. In fact, this might have been the first time.

"Are you ready?" Oliver asked as he took her hand.

Paige adjusted the flowers in her arm. "I'm nervous. Why am I so nervous?"

"Because next to you, she's the most important woman in my life."

And that was cause for her to take a few more breaths of cold air. "I'm important?"

Oliver turned to face her. "Yeah. Hasn't this week proven that?"

"We're not just sleeping together?"

Oliver's eyes narrowed. "Is that what you think is going on?"

"No," she said quickly. "No, I think my insides go all gooey when you look at me. I find every little tidbit of your past that you share with me turns me to mush. When I'm not with you all I can do is think of being with you."

"Yeah, that's what I'm talking about," he said smiling down at her.

"Next week is going to be a very long week."

"You'll be with your family celebrating your father. Don't give me another thought. C'mon, let's get inside. I need to come out and scoop off her walk and stairs."

"I can help."

"No. The reason it's not done yet is because she wants alone time with you."

Paige bit down on her lip. "She told you that?"

Oliver chuckled as he turned to walk toward the house. "I just know her that well. The boy next door would have already come over to ask to scoop it for her. I see his footprints. She normally would let him, and pay him a few dollars. She left this for me to get me out of the house."

Letting out a slow and steady breath, Paige tried to calm her nerves. She hoped his grandmother wasn't going to be disappointed.

Oliver knocked on the door and they waited for his grandmother to come to the door. When she appeared, Paige fell in love with her at first sight.

With a head full of white curls, and an apron covering her dress, her eyes sparkled behind her bifocals the moment she saw her grandson.

"Ollie, darling. And this is your beautiful girl?" she asked.

"Grandma, this is Paige Devereaux. Paige, this is my grandma, Iris."

Paige held out her cold and trembling hand. "It's nice to meet you."

Iris took her hand and covered it with her own. "Likewise. Come in. Ollie, will you see to the walk?"

Oliver winked at Paige. "Of course."

He turned and walked back outside, and Iris, with her hand still on Paige's guided her inside.

Paige handed her the flowers in her other hand. "These are for you."

Iris took the flowers and sniffed their fragrance. "These are delightful. C'mon, I have vases in the kitchen."

Oliver moved past the front window with the snow shovel in his hand and Paige felt the smile tug at her lips. Paige followed Iris to the kitchen where she took a vase out of the cupboard and set it on the counter.

"Sit, honey. Let's chat," Iris said as she laid the flowers on the table and pulled a pair of scissors from a jar on the table. She handed the scissors to Paige. "Help me open that little food packet."

Iris turned to retrieve the vase as Paige pulled out the packet of powder that would preserve the flowers. She cut it open as Iris filled the vase with flowers.

"I'm so glad to meet you. My Ollie talks highly of you and has for a long time."

Paige felt the heat rise in her cheeks. "That's very sweet."

"I worry about him working so hard, but I'm glad he's been taking some time off to be with you," she said turning with the vase of water.

Paige smiled as Iris sat across from her. The comment about him taking time to spend with her stuck with Paige. As close as he appeared to be with his grandmother, Oliver must not have mentioned the reason for his taking time off of work.

"It's been nice to spend time with him."

"I haven't been by this new tap house yet. Too many people," she laughed as she began to put flowers into the vase. "But it makes him happy to create places with his friends. Your sister is married to one of them, right?"

"Yes. Joel married my sister Kennedy."

"And now they have a little girl?"

"Matilda. She's one of the lights of my life."

"And you? Will you be wanting children?"

Paige felt her breath stick in her lungs as she formulated an answer. "Well, I haven't given children too much thought. I'm working on opening my own business right now, so I guess I'll have to see what the future brings."

The chilled air blew through the house and hit Paige a moment before Oliver walked into the kitchen. His nose was red from the cold, but his smile was wide and it warmed Paige.

"How are my best girls getting along?" he asked as he placed his hands on Paige's shoulders.

"Magnificently," Iris said. "I'm making her uncomfortable, and she hasn't cracked yet." She laughed as she added another flower to the vase.

Oliver gave Paige's shoulder a squeeze. "I should have warned you about her," he teased. "She's sorta protective of me."

Paige could tell that it went both ways. He might not have a relationship with his parents, but he'd always known he was loved, and it showed.

CHAPTER 27

As Paige walked among her students at her early morning class, she watched as they maneuvered through the forms. Like always, she'd help one student with foot placement and another with a deeper stretch. Only now, she kept her hands off of Oliver and simply admired his long, lean body as she passed by.

The morning class concluded with soft words and a mantra to carry her students for the day.

"Namaste," she said, opening her eyes and looking around the room.

Her regular students moved from their mats and began to roll them up. Oliver took his customary few moments of reflection and breath before rolling up his mat.

It was the last three students, the ones that never attended six o'clock class, that had Paige puzzled. They remained on their mats.

Paige noticed Oliver's glance in their direction and she nodded to him to meet her up front.

"I'll catch a ride with one of them," Paige said. "It appears I'm about to have an intervention of sorts."

Oliver ran his hand down her arm. "I can stay."

"They're harmless. Besides, if they want help on the airplane with crying toddlers on Wednesday, they're going to want to be nice to me."

He chuckled at that. "Call me if you need me."

Paige rose on her toes and kissed him. His beard tickled her lip, as he hadn't conditioned it to make it soft yet.

She waited for Oliver to walk out the door, and said goodbye to the rest of her students before she walked back to the studio. With her arms crossed in front of her, she narrowed her gaze on the three women still sitting on the floor.

Grabbing her own mat, she laid it back on the floor so that they were in a circle.

Meghann smiled sweetly, as Meghann would. Paige was used to her dropping into the class when she could. It always depended on the shooting schedule of her cooking show and her mother's health that day.

Kennedy hardly ever made it to a class, though Paige could sometimes convince her. But Hillary, she hadn't been since she'd become a mother.

Now the three of them sat on her floor quietly staring at her.

"Okay," she said. "Let me have it. You have more accusations? You have some wise married woman advice to give the kid? You need room in my suitcase to..."

"Knock it off," Kennedy said sharply. "Fine, we need to talk."

"Then have at it. I have a lunch time class, so let's not make this an all-day event," Paige snapped out the words, but noticed that no one flinched at them.

"First of all, I love you. We all love you."

"I know that."

"We're worried about you," Kennedy offered and Hillary rested a hand on Paige's thigh.

"You haven't been acting like yourself since you got involved with Oliver and..."

Paige held up a hand to cut Hillary off. "Wait, this isn't fair. Nothing has been normal since I hooked up with Oliver." She turned her attention to Kennedy. "It seems as if the moment I started hanging around him more, people started accusing him."

Kennedy took a breath to speak, but Meghann, with her braids falling in front of her shoulders, spoke first. "I think they want to make sure you're okay," she said. "You usually are at the tap house or at the store. You haven't been around much."

Though it was Meghann that spoke, Paige turned her attention back to Kennedy. "Let's see, when you start a relationship, you spend time with the guy. I don't know, sometimes you start staying at their house and sometimes you even lose track of time," Paige emphasized the words to remind Kennedy that she'd done the same thing when she'd started dating Joel.

"Difference was Joel was building something. Oliver is tearing it apart."

Now Paige's jaw trembled. "He hasn't been there in a week."

"It was a lot of money, Paige."

Paige stood. "I don't need this. I love him and I'm not going to let you do this. I thought that when I fell in love with a man my sister would be there to support me."

Kennedy stood and the other two followed.

"Paige, I do support you. I'm happy for you."

"But you can't be happy for us."

Kennedy's lips pursed. "I think we should focus on Dad's wedding, and then when we get back, we can focus on everything else."

"By the time we get back, there might not be anything left. Oliver might have stolen it all." Paige shouted.

"Now you're just picking more fights," Kennedy's voice shook now.

"I think you're the one that came in here to fight. You're not my mother and I'm a full grown adult. I'll make my decisions and I'll make some mistakes along the way. But Oliver isn't a mistake."

Hillary pushed between the sisters and shifted them each a stern look. "I've never seen the two of you fight like this. I think we're done here. Kennedy, you have a manicure appointment, so you should go. Paige, you need to put some peace back into your heart before that lunch class. Wednesday morning, we will pick everyone up to go to the airport. We're going to go in as a group, and we're going to support your dad and Gloria. We'll be on a freaking island with sun and sand, and I expect the two of you to be civil. Ken, she's not the one stealing from the tap house. If it's Oliver, it'll be found out and dealt with, but not at the expense of your relationship with your sister."

Paige could see Kennedy's shoulders drop.

Hillary turned her attention to Paige. "She may not be your mother, but she stepped in when she needed to and she's always had your back. That's never going to change."

Paige hated this feud that was happening between them.

Taking the initiative, she stepped forward and pulled Kennedy in for a hug.

"I'm okay, sis. He treats me so wonderfully, and I know in my heart I'm falling in love with him," she said in her sister's ear. "I don't think he's the one doing this, but if he is, I'll deal with that heartbreak. I'm a grown woman."

Kennedy pulled back, her eyes moist with tears. "I love you, Paige. I just want everyone happy again."

And Paige knew that. Kennedy was always their peacemaker. There was no reason that would change even in adulthood.

CHAPTER 28

Oliver reclined on Paige's bed, jeans and T-shirt clad, he crossed his ankles and watched as she filled her suitcase over and over.

"I thought you'd already decided what you were taking to Hawaii. Why are you going through everything again?" he asked as he tapped his fingers on his chest.

"I'm nervous. I redo things when I'm nervous."

"Nervous to fly? Nervous that your dad is making a mistake? Nervous that your SPF six hundred isn't going to be enough?"

Paige snorted a laugh when he said that and then shook her head. "My sister is worried about me because of the situation at the tap house," she blurted the words out and then dropped the dresses she had in her hand onto the bed. "Oliver, something is going on. They're blaming you, and in turn Kennedy is in my face about it because I'm sleeping with you."

Oliver sat up. "You're not just sleeping with me. Right? We've discussed this. There's more here."

"Yeah, there's more." She growled and picked up the pile of shirts she had laying on the bed and dumped them into the suitcase. "Just tell me you're not involved in the money missing from the tap house."

Oliver ran his tongue over his teeth and took his time to stand and walk to her. "I've told you that too."

"I know, but..."

"No, I've told you. Paige, if they're getting into your head and you're second guessing me, then how is this going to work?"

She could feel the sharp sting her doubt was having on both of them, and she turned and folded herself into his arms. "I'm sorry. I'm just worked up."

Oliver smoothed his hand over her hair and pressed a kiss to her forehead. "I know. We're going to get this all worked out. And the moment you get home, you're going to close on your business, and there'll be new challenges."

He was right. She'd be gone a week, and the day after she returned, she was going to close on her yoga studio. Things were going to work out.

"I think I should go home and let you do this," he said kissing her cheek. "You could use some time to process."

Paige shook her head. "No. Not now. It would probably be best if you weren't here in the morning when they come for me, but not yet."

Oliver placed his finger under her chin and lifted it so that she looked up at him. "I'm going to tell you something that I don't tell other people."

Paige's heart rate raced. What could he possibly be keeping inside him that he didn't say to anyone? Was he about to confess? God, was he really to blame? Her head began to spin and her breath caught in her lungs.

"Paige Devereaux, I love you."

Now she felt nearly faint, and her body swayed against his for support. "What?"

Oliver chuckled. "You heard me. I love you."

She finally was able to suck in a breath. "Oh. Wow. I didn't expect that."

"That's when it's the best, right? When you least expect it?"

Yeah, well she was sure he was going to spill his story, and this wasn't the story she'd been expecting. But hadn't she told her sister she loved him too?

"Oliver, wow, um..."

"Don't say anything. I took you off guard. I just felt very strongly about this and..."

"I love you too," she let the words fall out before she could reconsider them and worry over the. "I do. I love you too."

His lips turned into a wide grin. "Well, now we've opened a whole new can of worms." He looked down at the pile of clothes on her bed. "Let's get you packed. I want one more night with you before you go. I'll be gone before midnight," he promised.

At eleven fifty-eight, Paige kissed Oliver goodnight and watched as he drove away from her house. It would be the last time she'd see him for a week. For the next seven days, she'd be with her family only—the same family that wasn't too keen on her relationship with him.

They were gracious, and she knew she didn't have to worry about what would happen. It would all be okay.

Paige turned off the lights in her living room and headed to the kitchen for a glass of water. She pulled a glass from the cupboard and walked to the refrigerator to fill it, but stopped when she saw the note and the check on the door, secured with a magnet.

You owe me thirty-five thousand dollars. No interest. No penalties for early or late payments. Free yoga classes must be included.

She laughed at that and set the glass on the counter because she needed to wipe the tears that had begun to sting her eyes.

I believe in what you're building, and I want to be there for it. I love you, Paige. Have a wonderful vacation. I'll be here when you get back.

Love, Oliver

Behind the note was a check for the amount she needed to secure the purchase of the studio.

Her hand shook as she looked down at the check. He believed in her.

She hurried back to her bedroom, nearly tripping over the suitcase on the floor. Picking up her phone she texted him.

Thank you, was all she sent.

A few minutes later he texted back. *I love you. I believe in you. I'll see you soon.*

Paige dropped down on her bed and laid back. His scent still lingered on her sheets. She held the note and the check to her chest. It was all going to be okay. Everyone would see in him what she saw. Oliver Westcott was a good and decent man, and the love of her life, apparently.

She laughed as she got up and tucked the check into her purse. They were going to pick her up at six in the morning, but she'd drive over to the bank at five and put the check into the ATM.

CHAPTER 29

Paige had risen at four o'clock—nervous about travel, what she'd packed, and the check in her purse. She hadn't slept well.

After showering, pulling her hair up, and getting dressed, she sat at her kitchen table and fretted over the check. When she'd found it the night before, she'd been excited about what it offered. Now, hovering a pen over the deposit slip, the thought of putting it in the bank made her sick.

Max had agreed to give her the money. It would be wiser to accept his offer than to put the check she held in her hand in the bank.

Paige's eyes burned from lack of sleep, but the pre-travel energy buzzed in her veins. She could sit on the sofa and wait for her ride. Closing her eyes would be the smart thing to do, and so would putting the check away and not cashing it.

Then, her phone buzzed in her hand, startling her.

Cash the damn check, the text read, and was soon followed by a laughing emoji. *I know you're going to fret over it. I want to do this.*

Paige laughed, and even looked around to see if he were

watching her through a window. *How did you know I was fretting over it?* She replied.

Because I love you. She focused on that line. Holding her phone to her chest, she thought about him saying it for the first time. And then her phone buzzed again. *Have a safe trip. Let me know when you get there.*

It was decided. She'd run the check to the bank and put it in the ATM. Now she would fret over that too. At least she could call Amy, who worked at the bank and took her classes regularly, to make sure it got handled. Then, when she returned from Hawaii, everything would be in place for her to close on the business as she and Pricilla had planned. Her week away would give Pricilla plenty of time to get everything in order.

AT QUARTER TO SIX, one of Chase's limousines pulled up in front of her house, and Chase climbed from the back and hurried up her front steps. Paige had been nursing a cup of coffee, sitting at the front window waiting for them.

She stood as soon as the car pulled up, opened the door, and hurried to the kitchen to pour out her coffee.

"You look wide awake," Chase said as he picked up her suitcase.

Paige pulled on her coat and zipped it up. "I've been up for a few hours."

She grabbed her purse from the chair, turned off the lights, and locked the door behind her.

Chase carried her suitcase to the car, and the man he had driving the car stood ready to open the door for her.

She thanked him and climbed into the back where her entire family already sat under the blue hue of the light that ran the length of the car.

"Good morning," she said softly.

Meghann was the first to speak. "Good morning. You're very chipper this early."

"I've been up a few hours. I'm sure I'll sleep on the plane."

Paige settled in next to Kennedy, and a sleepy Matilda.

When Matilda finally lifted her head to look at her aunt, she reached for Paige. Paige took the sleepy toddler and held her against her as Matilda fell asleep on her shoulder.

"I do think you're her favorite," Kennedy said as she rubbed her hand down her daughter's back.

There was some strain in her voice, though Paige was sure Kennedy didn't even know it was there. And, it hadn't gone unnoticed that when she sat down next to Kennedy, Joel had looked the other way. Maybe while they were in Hawaii, and far from the tap house, she could have a chat with him. She loved and believed in Oliver, and she supposed that Joel's biggest problem was that he did too. There was a leak in his organization, but Paige didn't truly believe that he thought it was Oliver.

PAIGE HAD BEEN the last one to be picked up because she was the closest to the airport, even if it was still another forty-five minutes away. The drive was mostly quiet, and any conversations were held in whispers because it was early. Meghann had taken a phone call from the facility that her mother lived in. Paige had rested a hand on hers when she could see whatever news they had given her had upset her slightly.

Though the timing wasn't ideal, Paige thought maybe their father had been on to something by having a destination wedding and expecting them all to be there. They could all use the time away, together.

As they pulled up at the airport, and through to departures, the car stopped at the first airline where she and Kennedy's family would get out. The others were booked on different airlines.

Joel stepped out of the car and then turned to take the sleeping toddler from Paige's arms. Then, he offered her a hand to help her from the car.

"Thank you," she said softly and he smiled. Perhaps there was hope for them yet.

The airport was beginning to bustle to life as they checked in, made their way through security, and headed toward the gate.

"I need to take Matilda and get her changed," Kennedy said as she pulled the diaper bag up onto her shoulder and hoisted her daughter onto her hip. A moment later she walked away leaving Paige and Joel alone.

"I'll be glad to have some sunshine," Paige began. "I'm over the gray skies we've had lately."

Joel nodded. "It'll be a peaceful trip."

"I'm going to meet my step siblings, I guess. That feels weird."

"If they're as wonderful as Gloria says they are, you'll be fine," Joel said, and even smiled.

"Are you going to be okay with me?" She had to ask, though she hadn't thought she would until they had landed.

Joel let out a breath and covered her hand with his, giving it a squeeze. "I love Oliver," he said and Paige nodded.

"So do I."

Joel took a moment. "That's where you're at? You're in love?"

Paige turned so that she was facing him. "I am. I know this hurts you, but..."

"What hurts me is the uncertainty. He says he didn't do it, and part of me believes him. But right now, there just isn't any proof."

"I think you should look into your bookkeeper," she said easing back in her seat. "Seriously, you've been with Oliver a long time. Why would he do this to you?"

Joel let out a breath. "That's what keeps spinning in my head. I don't want to worry about this while we're gone."

"Then don't," Paige said easily. "Nothing is going to happen that your brother and Craig can't handle until we get back. Enjoy your family. Enjoy my family," she teased. "And, Joel, I do have your back too."

He gave her hand another squeeze. She knew he understood.

CHAPTER 30

Oliver sat in his car outside the tap room and drummed his fingers on the steering wheel. There was a small Wednesday lunch rush, which was the norm when the sandwich truck was there.

It had been almost a week since he'd set foot in the tap house, but he owned a fourth of the business. It was all equal in owner-ship, the brothers had just won the coin toss all those years ago for the naming rights. He should have the right to go in and take part in his shift, and in his business.

With Joel out of town, it would be one less person in his way. Not that Joel was the problem, and Oliver knew that. In spirit, they were all brothers. He knew that none of them thought he would turn on them, but he needed to prove that he still thought the business—and their relationship—was important.

Oliver finally opened the car door and stepped out onto the gravel. Closing the door, he sucked in a breath, and headed toward the back door when it swung open and Craig stepped outside holding two empty crates.

He stood in front of Oliver looking at him as if maybe he'd seen a ghost.

"Craig."

"What are you doing here?" Craig asked letting the door close behind him.

"It's my shift."

"This shift started at ten. It's noon."

"Took me a bit to gather the courage to come," he admitted as Craig set the crates in the pile near the door.

As Craig turned back, he tucked his hands into his front pockets and studied Oliver. "I thought you were going to take some time off."

"I did. I know you all want me to take more time, but seriously, a fourth of this business is mine. There is no reason for me not to be here."

The door opened again and Jeff stepped outside. "I saw you guys on the camera. What's going on?"

Craig exchanged glances with Oliver before stepping closer to Jeff. "He says he's come to work his shift."

Jeff nodded. "I thought you were going to take some time."

Oliver stepped closer to the two men that created a wall in front of the door, though he didn't assume they were purposely keeping him out. "I'm tired of time off. This is my business too, and I want to work. If you're worried I'm going to steal, then someone else work the money. Shit, I'll bus and clean. I don't care. I want to be part of what I helped build. I'm not taking anything. I haven't taken anything."

"What about Joel?" Jeff asked.

"He's on a plane. I'm not going around him. I'm just looking to do what I enjoy most, which is working with you guys."

Craig bit down on his lip. "You're not stealing from us?"

"No. I have never taken anything from you guys, except for the money you lay on the table when we play darts."

Jeff laughed. "I still don't know how you can hit that many bullseyes in a row."

Oliver took a few more steps toward his partners. "If money

is disappearing, then I think I need to be in on it too. Seriously, I would never hurt any of you. You're my brothers."

Jeff exchanged glances with Craig, and then he moved toward Oliver his hand extended. "You are a brother," Jeff said shaking Oliver's hand and then pulling him in for a hug. "Let's figure this out all together and make the bleeding stop."

Oliver eased out of the hug. "Is it that bad?"

"It made a hefty dent," Jeff said as he put his hand on Oliver's shoulder. "Let's get back in there and get to work."

Jeff might have been accepting and ready to get back to work, but Oliver had seen the doubt shadow Craig's eyes. He wasn't out of the woods yet. They wanted to trust him, but the truth was, they didn't yet. He'd change that.

"When we close out, we all do it together. I don't mind you all looking over my shoulder."

Jeff nodded. "Let's get to work."

OLIVER WAS at home behind the bar, and though he hadn't been away from it for long, his heart was full—well almost. He checked his phone regularly hoping that Paige would text him when she landed. If she were sitting at the bar while he worked his shift, that would completely fill his heart.

"It's nice to see you here, finally," a woman's voice drew Oliver's attention from his phone.

His mother sat down at the bar near his station. Her blonde hair was piled in curls atop her head and a pair of earrings dangled from her ears. There was a signature pink stone in the earrings, which told him where she'd purchased them. Laying her hands flat on the bar, he noticed the long red fingernails, and that ring.

"What are you doing here?"

"I came for a beer. There is a citrus one I really liked the last time I was in here," she said looking at the board behind him. "Fast and fruit, yeah, that's the one."

Oliver chewed the inside of his cheek. "I think you should go."

His mother shook her head. "I may have not been a very good mother—"

"Or one at all," he added, his voice hushed to keep their conversation as private as possible.

His mother's eyes grew moist and he thought that should have affected him, but it didn't. It was the truth, and she should have known it too.

"Oliver, I'm trying to get to know you."

Against his better judgement, and perhaps only because Craig had walked behind him, Oliver poured the beer and slid it in front of his mother.

"I didn't ask you to come here and get to know me. In fact, my grandmother looked almost petrified to have you in her home."

His mother twisted the ring on her finger, which he had to assume was a nervous habit. "Please. Will you just give me some time?"

Oliver's phone buzzed on the bar and he noticed Paige's beautiful face appear on the screen, but so had his mother.

He picked up the phone and looked at the text. *Settled into my hotel room. Off to dinner with everyone soon. I miss you already. Can't wait till I'm home. I love you.*

Oliver tucked his phone in his pocket and turned back to his mother smiling at him.

"She's pretty," his mother said. "I saw the picture."

"She is pretty."

"Wife?"

"I'm sure you've done enough investigating, that you know exactly who she is."

His mother took a long drink from her beer. "I just wanted to know about my son."

Oliver filled another order, filed the money into the cash

drawer, and turned to his mother. "Breakfast on Saturday. Molly's Diner on the other side of the square. This is my one offer for you to sit with me and talk."

His mother batted her eyes to keep the tears that had formed from falling. "Thank you, Ollie."

"One time. I've lived a very nice life and I don't regret a moment of it. Grandma raised me to be a gracious man who works hard and doesn't need for anything. None of that is going to change."

His mother nodded. "I understand. Saturday morning will be fine."

CHAPTER 31

Paige stepped out of her room and heard the whistle. She turned to see her father walking toward her and she hurried to him.

"Dad," she said on a laugh. "I didn't know your room was up here."

He put his arm around Paige's shoulder as they walked toward the elevators. "I got the honeymoon suite for after the wedding, but I didn't tell Gloria that. I wanted to surprise her."

"That's very sweet." Paige pushed the button to call the elevator. "Where is Gloria?"

"She's with her kids. They'll meet us for dinner. You look beautiful, by the way."

Paige looked at herself in the shiny metal door of the elevator. The sundress was something she'd bought off her sister's clearance rack last spring, and she hadn't had the opportunity to wear it yet. The fact that it was November, and she had it on, thrilled her. She couldn't wait until they spent the day on the beach. She would finally feel as if she were on vacation.

The elevator arrived and the doors opened. Paige and her father stepped inside and rode to the lobby. When the doors opened again, she saw her entire family gathered together. Her father wrapped his arm around her shoulders again, and they walked toward the rest of their family.

Paige watched as their father hugged and kissed everyone, and took little Kennedy and hoisted her up on his hip.

As they all started toward the front doors of the hotel, Kennedy moved in next to Paige.

"Joel said that Oliver went back to work," she said in a hushed tone.

"I thought they wanted him to take time away."

Kennedy hooked her arm with Paige's. "He said he showed up and asked to work."

"I guess that's positive, right?"

Kennedy smiled. "Sounds positive to me."

THEIR FATHER and Gloria had arranged to have a private room at the restaurant. The bank of windows looked out over the ocean and Paige found her attention directed outside often.

Gloria's family was as delightful as she'd said they were. It was easy to spend hours at the restaurant listening to Gloria and her father talk about life in Florida, and her children talking about growing up with Gloria as their mother. As usual, the Devereaux siblings tended to be less vocal about their upbringing, since their father's infidelity had torn apart many families.

Paige had been born nearly a decade after her father had the affair that changed the course of his family. Kennedy's mother had been pregnant when Chase's mother became pregnant as well. Their father had gone back to his wife and Max was born. However, in the end, two marriages ended.

Paige was born into a loving marriage, and the thought that her father had ever done something so deceitful still didn't seem real to her. He'd doted on her Paige's entire life, especially when her mother was killed. Now, Paige watched as he gazed into

Gloria's eyes. There was true love there, and it made her miss Oliver.

Then, as if he knew she was thinking of him, her phone rang.

Paige excused herself and stepped out onto the balcony. The warm, fresh air swirled around her, and the water lapping at the rocks gave her peace.

"I miss you," she answered.

"I miss you, too," Oliver replied. "How are things going?"

"Wonderful, so far. We just had dinner."

"And your new step-siblings?" he asked with a laugh.

"They're as nice as Gloria said." Paige leaned against the railing. "I heard you went back to work."

There was a moment of silence on the other end of the phone before Oliver spoke. "I did. Ballsy move, but thought it needed to be made. I own a fourth of the company. They can't keep me out." She heard him let out a breath. "They were gracious about it. It was nice to be back."

His voice had shaken slightly, and it made her wonder if things weren't as calm as he tried to make it sound. "Did something happen?"

"Just a patron sitting at the bar got under my skin."

"Were they causing problems?"

"No. Anyway, it's not important. Is it warm there?" he asked.

Paige looked out over the water and let the warm breeze blow through her hair. "It's so beautiful. I've heard they have yoga retreats here, and I think I'll come back for one."

"That sounds delightful. I should let you get back to your family. Have fun, Paige."

"I love you," she said softly.

"I love you too."

Paige disconnected the phone call, then she leaned against the railing and looked out over the water. The surroundings were peaceful, and Paige appreciated its calming effects on her body. God, couldn't she stay right there for the rest of the week?

When the door opened, Gloria stepped through. She had two glasses of champagne, and she handed one to Paige.

"Everything okay?" she asked.

Paige took the glass. "Everything is fine. Just taking a phone call."

Gloria leaned against the railing next to Paige. was. "I've worried about you and my marriage to your father," Gloria said before she took a sip of her champagne. "I know that he loved your mother very much, and you are his world, well, all of you are." She took another sip. "But you were the one that was all his. He never had to share you with an ex-wife, or an ex-lover." Her voice trailed off when she said it.

"You know all the details, don't you?"

Gloria nodded. "He's so proud of all you kids. He knows he messed things up, but he says he did the best he could to amend what he could."

"And it doesn't scare you away?"

Gloria laughed. "A man in his twenties is a much different man than a man facing his sixties." She sipped her drink again. "I hear you're seeing one of Joel's business partners."

So there had been some gossip among family members, she thought. Of course, there was.

"Yes. Oliver."

"The one with the very nice beard?"

Paige laughed. "That's him. I can't even keep my hair that soft."

"He seems like a nice man."

Okay, so maybe they hadn't gossiped completely. Wouldn't she question him too if she thought he'd been stealing from Joel?

"I guess I should get back inside. Are you going to join us?"

"Yes." Paige followed Gloria back inside to the room where the mix of families laughed and shared stories.

CHAPTER 32

The shift was over, and both Jeff and Craig had stayed until the end. When it was time to close out the drawer, Oliver handed it over to them.

"Let's do it together," he said. "Watch how I do it."

"You don't have to do this," Jeff said.

"Yes, I do. I need to close this drawer just like I close it every shift. And then, when you get your fancy report back from the bookkeeper, we'll compare."

Craig shook his head. "You think that a professional is going to lie?"

"I think your professional is lying. I didn't have any input on who we used for bookkeeping." When he saw that Jeff took a breath to argue, Oliver continued. "I know. I didn't care. I remember the conversation. I didn't put input into it. I trusted the process."

The three men took the cash drawer to the office and balanced it, just as they would any other night. They agreed on all of the numbers, bagged up the cash, printed the paperwork, and Jeff picked up the pen to sign the sheets.

"No," Oliver interrupted him. "I'll sign it. You both were here.

You both can verify this. Take a picture of it. I want proof that you both see the numbers that are here."

Jeff took his phone from his pocket and snapped the picture.

Oliver signed the form that said he had been the one to close out the drawer. Then, they sealed up the bag, and put it into the safe.

The bookkeeping service would come and take the deposits every weekday. He'd have to wait to see if something was amiss, but now the other two were in on it. They had proof that the cash in the bag matched the numbers on the sheet.

SATURDAY MORNING, Oliver parked his car on the side of Molly's Diner. His palms were damp and there was an ache in his jaw from clenching it.

He'd promised his mother he'd meet with her, but he had begun to regret his decision the moment he'd made the offer. There was nothing the woman could do for him. He was thirty-one years old. He'd had twenty-three years to process the fact that after his grandparents had come for him, his parents had never come back.

It hadn't been a hard decision to leave with his grandparents that day. His father had been gone for a week, which was normal, and his mother had been passed out, face down, on the floor when he walked out of that teepee for the last time.

At that moment, he missed his grandfather something terrible. And he was over grateful for his grandmother, who had told him that she adored Paige.

Families were a mixed up lot, he thought as he climbed from his car. He knew the history of Paige's family, and his was equally as unique a story.

When he walked through the front door of Molly's, he saw his mother in a corner booth. Her hair was down today, and grazed her shoulders. A full face of makeup, beautiful clothes, and a purse that she held in her lap which probably cost more than his car. Hadn't she gone full circle from the woman that lived in a teepee, took drugs to free her mind, and left her child shoeless and with a lack of education?

When she looked up at him, her eyes were wide with gratitude. He recognized that look from the one his grandmother always gave him.

"Ollie, I'm so glad you showed. I wasn't sure," his mother began. "I got here early. I didn't want to miss you."

"I told you I'd be here," he said as he sat down. "I keep my promises." It might have been a dig at her, but he just didn't care.

"You did. I was glad to see you at work the other night. You're very good with people."

"I enjoy my job."

"It shows."

The server came to their table, and in order to hurry though the meal, Oliver ordered a bowl of fruit and a cup of tea without ever looking at the menu. His mother scrambled to order a meal, which he had a feeling he'd be paying for.

"So, tell me about this girl you're seeing. I hear..."

"Mom, I don't want to talk about her," Oliver cut her off. "Let's talk about why you're here. Why did you come to find me twenty-three years later? You've never come around before."

His mother gripped her purse tighter. "Ollie, please don't get mad at me. I didn't know where to..."

"You knew where to find me. You knew right where I was the whole time."

"Well, to get back here, that took some work."

"Right. Did you walk from San Francisco? That's the only way it might have taken twenty-three years."

Her lip trembled, but he couldn't help it. How was he supposed to control himself around her and be cordial?

"Your father..."

"Disappeared. I know that. I know he was missing when I left."

"Well, when he did come back, he came back with another family. I never really understood if it was his family or not. Times then were so confusing."

"Drugs will do that to you, Mom. You were face down on the floor and my father was missing. Did you ever wonder why Grandpa and Grandma came for me?"

A tear rolled down her cheek. "I knew why. I think I was angry that they didn't take me with you. They left me there."

He'd never, ever, considered that.

"Would you have gone with us?" Oliver asked.

His mother bit down on her lip, carrying the lipstick to her teeth as she did so. "I don't know. Probably not. I would have probably run away with you again."

At least at this point in her life she could be honest about it.

"Ollie, all I can offer you is an apology. Your dad died and I was alone..."

"He died? I've never heard that. You said you hadn't seen him for eighteen years."

"That's right. He'd come and go. I'd become part of another family and he'd come back. One night he wandered into the bay and washed up later."

The thought had Oliver cringing. Was his death as nondescript as that? No one deserved to die like that. No child ever deserved to hear about it.

"Let's just skip all of that. Let's talk about why you're here now, dressed like you are, and that ring. Let's talk about that ring."

CHAPTER 33

Oliver's mother took a deep breath and looked at the ring on her finger. "I've been married to Mason for ten years. I met him in a shelter when he was doing volunteer work, community service," she added, or corrected. He wasn't sure. "They had cleaned us all out of the park, again, and that was where I ended up. He'd been an alcoholic and lost his family too."

Oliver wasn't sure this guy was much better than his own father, but looking at his mother, they must have done okay.

She continued, "He was doing his community service hours at the shelter after having caused an accident. Of course he got a DUI and did some time."

He knew she was searching his eyes for disgust, but Oliver worked to keep his face neutral as the server brought their breakfast. He figured he'd give her until he was done eating to finish her story.

"We stayed in contact for a few years. Then when he was free from his service obligations, he came to find me. He wanted to leave California and start somewhere new. I suggested we come here."

Oliver stabbed a grape and put it in his mouth, snapping his teeth against the fork. "You've been here for ten years?"

His mother batted her eyes. "Eight. Ollie, I wanted to give you a life free from me. You deserved that." She paused and took a breath. "For the record, you didn't seek me out either."

Nope, that much was true. And had he, what would he have done if he'd found her living in the same city?

If she'd been that close, for the past eight years, had she kept tabs on him? Did she know everything about his life? Had she been spying on him and his grandmother?

Oliver sipped his tea. He wanted to be calm so that she knew that none of this was getting to him, but he wasn't sure how much longer he could hold it all in.

"So why are you here now? Why after all this time did you decide now is a good time to seek me out?"

She bit down on her lip again, and now the lipstick was nearly gone. "We've fallen on hard times. I just felt as if I needed my family around me. I'm human, Ollie."

And greedy, he thought. "I'm sorry you're having a hard time."

"Mason works hard, he really does. I work with him from time to time, but I'm no good with numbers. In fact, I'm not much good at anything. Though, that little dress shop near your bar, I think I could work there."

Had she not done enough digging? Did he know who owned that dress shop and how it involved him? If she didn't, he wasn't going to mention it. But when Kennedy returned, he'd sure as hell mention it to her. The last thing Kennedy needed was his mother as an employee.

"You're looking for financial help?" he asked, deciding it was better to cut to the chase than to let her just continue on the way she was.

"I'd also like to know my son."

Sure she did, he thought.

"I don't know what kind of help you need, but I can't help you."

"Oliver, I know how well you're doing in your business."

Well, at least she'd used his real name, he thought.

"The business is good. It's been good for years. You know this is the second tap house we've built. We sold the other, and that netted us nicely."

He watched her lips purse now. "But you won't help me?"

"You're not a very good detective are you?" He pushed away his fruit and his tea. "If you were, you'd know that suddenly we're losing money and my partners think I'm stealing it."

Her eyes went wide and she loosened the grip on her purse.

"Yeah, that's right. The reason I hadn't been at work was because they asked me to stay away."

"But you must have some savings. You don't own anything but that house and that car," she said pleading.

Oh, she was a piece of work. "For your information, I just invested in a new business. My savings are depleted." And that was all she needed to know. "I'm sorry for you and your husband," he said pulling his wallet out of his pocket and picking up the ticket the server had left. He would have just put the money down, but in the state of mind his mother was in, he wasn't sure that was wise. He'd pay at the front and tip the server personally.

As he started out of the booth, his mother looked up at him. "Ollie, please. I think Mason is in some kind of trouble."

"Maybe you should look into the community resources that are available. There are shelters. There are financial aid options. Mom, I have my own problems. I can't focus on you right now."

She called after him once more, but Oliver kept walking. He might not win any awards for son-of-the-year, but then he'd never been treated like a son. As the door closed on the diner, he walked to his car, climbed in, and drove away as quickly as he could.

He headed toward the lake to walk around it a few times before heading to the tap house. If his mother showed up, he'd call the police.

As Oliver sat at the first light, his signal on to turn left, he thought better about it and got into the other lane. Perhaps he'd better stop by his grandmother's house first. She needed to know what had happened, and that his mother had been in town for years. For the first time in his life, he didn't feel safe leaving his grandmother alone in her house.

Surely there would be an argument about it, but he could deal with that. If he had to take her to work with him all night, he'd do it.

As he drove toward her house he actually laughed at that thought. Maybe he'd make more in tips if his grandmother was sitting at the bar in her apron.

CHAPTER 34

Paige rose early on Monday morning. Though she wasn't in her own studio, she could still get her practice in. After all, she'd spent most of Sunday in bed in the hotel room, hungover from the wedding reception that had gone on into early Sunday morning.

Her father was happy, and that made her happy.

She opened her laptop, and of course was sucked into her email before she could cue up her music. She couldn't stand to see there were messages waiting to be read, and it distracted her every time.

Determined to just scan the emails, assuming they were Monday morning shopping specials from the many email lists she belonged to, she started to scroll.

There was one email from Pricilla with the date and time on Thursday for the closing on the business. Her heart raced as she read it. By the end of the week, the wellness center would be hers, and she could start to transform it.

Her eyes began to sting with tears. Why was she going to cry? That was exactly what she wanted. Finally, just like her sister and brothers, she'd have something that was her own. She owed Oliver a great deal of that gratitude.

Max had promised to start work on the space the following week. It was always good to have talented siblings.

The next email that caught her eye was from Amy at the bank. She wanted to let Paige know that it was taking longer than normal for the check to credit to her account, reaffirming that checks of that size usually took a few days. Paige had expected that, but she hoped that it would all clear by Wednesday so that she could get the cashier's check made to give to Pricilla for the sale.

Paige emailed Amy back hoping to offer herself some peace of mind that the check would be deposited before Wednesday when she would come for the cashier's check.

Oliver had been gracious to give her the full amount, which she had decided would give her an opportunity to use what she had saved to better the center and get her studio up and running just the way she wanted.

Once the email was sent, Paige turned on her playlist and began her practice on the mat.

AFTER BREAKFAST, Oliver had gone straight to his grandmother's house, but she'd shooed him away with his silliness that she could be in danger. She could handle herself, she'd told him.

He wouldn't argue with her. Perhaps she'd been looking over her shoulder since the moment they'd taken him home.

From his grandmother's house he decided to head to the tap house.

Oliver parked behind the tap house. As he climbed from his car, Jeff came out the back door, and headed straight for him.

"I saw you drive up on the camera," Jeff said. "You're not scheduled."

Oliver nodded. "Just had breakfast with my mother. I needed to be somewhere else," he said and Jeff winced.

"Your mom?"

"Yeah."

"To be honest with you. I kinda thought your mom was dead."

That caused Oliver to chuckle. "I can see why you'd think that. But she's alive and financially in trouble. What a freaking mess of a time for her to come after me to get me to give her money."

"That's why I hurried out here. We need to talk," Jeff said.

"What's up?"

Jeff handed him a stack of papers. "This is the bookkeeping report. Your shift came out short."

Oliver lifted his eyes to Jeff. "You closed that drawer out with me. You watched me sign it. You verified the numbers."

Jeff nodded. "I think you're right. Something is up with the bookkeeping."

"Then let's figure it out."

"Joel will be here Wednesday. We're just not going to sign your name on anything. But if we find out that something is up with the bookkeeper, then we owe you a big apology."

They did, Oliver thought. "You can worry about that later. Have you talked to Joel?"

"Not yet. I wanted to show you first."

Oliver nodded. "Well, I guess we'd better get back inside and make up what was lost."

Jeff nodded, putting his arm around Oliver's shoulders. "You're right. Time to get to work."

Oliver followed Jeff though the back door and saw the sympathetic glance that Craig gave him from behind the bar. Sure, they were all sorry they'd accused him. Of course, Craig had nearly gone to blows with him.

He wasn't out of the woods yet. So, their plan had worked to give them a benchmark that someone was messing with his numbers. The curiosity was, why his numbers only, from the deposits bearing his signature?

"We got a new one tapped," Craig said to obviously break the ice between them. "New stout."

"I'll try it," he said walking behind the bar and taking down a glass.

"Hey, bro, I'm sorry. I mean, well shit. I'm just sorry."

Oliver placed a hand on Craig's shoulder. "We're not out of this yet. We need to find out where it's all going."

"I think Jeff and Joel plan to go talk to them when Joel gets back."

"Sounds like it. Hopefully this can get tied up and we won't have to worry about it anymore. I have other avenues I'd like to continue to explore," Oliver said as he moved to the tap with the new beer.

"You and Joel's sister-in-law?"

"Yeah." Oliver took a sip of the beer. "This is good."

"It'll be a fave. So tell me about you and Paige," Craig prodded as he leaned against the bar.

"It's been building since we opened. Now it's a serious thing."

"Serious."

"Serious," Oliver said again. "I can't wait until she gets home."

Craig watched him drink the beer and then moved toward the register and picked up a business card that was propped up against the screen. "A woman came in here this morning, right before we opened. she was looking for you. Blonde with a fancy purse."

Oliver swallowed hard. "Seriously?"

"Yeah. She looked distraught. She said she'd really like you to call her."

Craig handed Oliver the card. Every muscle in his body tensed when he saw his mother's name on the card. Hadn't he just talked to the woman and told her he wasn't going to help her? She was going to become problematic, he knew it.

CHAPTER 35

As the tires made contact with the runway, Paige batted her eyes open. It had been a long and delightful week, but she was glad to be home.

In a few hours she would be asleep in her own bed, and that had always been the reward for long hours of travel.

"Will you hold her for a moment?" Kennedy asked as she shifted her daughter from her lap to Paige's. "I hope she sleeps all night. But I have a feeling that's not going to happen."

Paige kissed her niece on the top of the head. "You'll let your mama sleep, right?" she teased. "Are you planning on going into work tomorrow?"

Kennedy tucked items that had been used to occupy her daughter back into her bag. "I'm sure I will. I don't suppose I'll be of any use though."

Paige chuckled. "I'm so excited to close on the business. Max better be prepared, I'm going to want to renovate it all."

"I'm happy for you, Paige. Just one more Devereaux taking over in this town."

"That's right."

Chase had arranged to have a car there to pick them up.

When the car pulled up in front of Paige's house she saw Oliver sitting on her front step.

"It looks like someone missed you," Joel whispered as Paige collected her purse.

"I missed him."

"Hey, I know there's been some stress, but he's a good guy."

Paige thought she might burst into tears hearing him say that. She'd worried that the rift between Joel and Oliver might be permanent.

"He is." Paige leaned in and hugged her brother-in-law before hugging her sister and kissing her niece on the head.

The driver held out his hand to help her from the car. Oliver stood as she stepped out. She took her suitcase from the driver and started up the front walk.

"I'm so glad to see you," she said as Oliver moved to her and wrapped his arms around her.

"Not nearly as glad as I am to see you." He pressed his cold lips to hers and she leaned in against him as the car pulled away from the curb. "Paige, I love you. I hope you don't mind that I'm sitting here waiting for you."

"I don't mind at all. Let's go inside. It's too cold to stand out here."

Oliver took her suitcase and followed her up the step. Paige took out her keys, unlocked the door, and stepped inside.

The moment they were inside the house, and the door had been closed to the outside world, Paige pushed Oliver up against the door and opened her mouth to his.

Oliver's hands slid over her bottom and Paige moaned.

"C'mon," she said taking his hand and pulling him toward her bedroom. "It's been a long week."

~

Oliver felt Paige stir, his arm still wrapped around her. They hadn't fallen asleep until early in the morning.

"What time is it?" Oliver asked, his eyes still closed.

"Seven."

"I'm going to need a lot of coffee today," he joked. "But so worth it. It's been a long week."

Paige rolled to face him. "You were quiet about your week. What made it so long?"

"I wanted you to enjoy your week. By the way, your tan is exquisite."

Paige laughed. "You haven't even seen me in the light yet."

"I can feel it."

"My dad is happy and in love with a wonderful woman. I spent the week on beaches and hiking with my entire family. Maybe the warmth of my tan comes from inside."

"Maybe. And you'll get to close on your business too."

"The sun just keeps shining."

He wasn't sure about that. It seemed as if for the past few weeks he'd been walking under a thundercloud, and he was just waiting to be struck by lightning.

"And," she rolled so that she straddled him, "you changed the subject. Tell me about your week."

Oliver ran his hands down her arms. "You're hovering over me all naked, and you want me to tell you why I had a long week?"

She bent and kissed him. "Okay, I'll go make some coffee and start some breakfast. When you're ready, meet me in the kitchen."

Paige eased off the bed, pulled on her robe, and walked out of the bedroom.

Oliver tucked his hands behind his head and took a moment to think about his week. It had been crap, plain and simple, minus the moment when Jeff and Craig thought they might owe him an apology.

Deciding the only way to get over it was to face it, Oliver sat up and swung his legs over the edge of the bed. Scrubbing his hands over his face, he stood and pulled on his pants. Paige might as well know what had been happening. There was a warning he needed to give her regarding his mother, and she needed to know if she was involved with him, chances were she'd cross his mother at some point.

Taking his time, he walked to the kitchen where Paige had turned on music, started the coffee brewing, and stood at the counter cutting up fruit. She was absolutely beautiful standing there in her robe, her hair piled atop her head, and the glow of that tan now evident.

"I had some bagels that were still good, but I'm out of cream cheese. Do you prefer butter or something else on yours?"

"I love you, Paige," he said causing her to stop what she was doing and look up at him.

She chuckled. "I love you too." She set the knife down and turned to look at him. "Everything okay?"

"I think it is. I just wanted you to know how I felt."

"I do know how you feel. It was the tone that worried me."

Oliver moved to her and rested his hands on her hips. "Do you think about forever?"

"In what terms?"

He raised his hand to her cheek and gazed into those dark eyes. "With a partner. You just came back from your dad's wedding. A marriage is forever. Do you think about that?"

Paige eased back. "Of course. All of my siblings have gotten married in the past two years and had babies. It's in my face."

"I've never thought of it," he admitted and he saw confusion swim in her eyes.

"Then why are you talking about it?"

"Because standing here watching you in your robe and waking up with you in the mornings, I can feel the need for it now."

Now Paige broke contact and went back to cutting grapes in

halves. "Why don't we have this discussion later. I think now that it's out there, we need to wrap our heads around it."

She was right. That had been foolish of him to even bring it up. What if he told her about his week and she decided she didn't want to be involved in that?

Instead of saying anything else, Oliver took mugs from the cupboard and filled them with coffee. There was no rush, he reminded himself. But his heart kept trying to change his mind.

CHAPTER 36

Paige carried the bowl of fruit, and two forks, to the table. There was a strange tension between them now, and she wasn't sure how she felt about that. Had he been trying to ask her to marry him? Or, what if he was feeling things out because he didn't want to marry her.

She sat down and immediately Oliver took her hand. "I didn't mean to freak you out," he said as he rubbed his thumb over her knuckles.

"I didn't say it freaked me out."

"You didn't have to say it." He took a breath and let it out slowly. "I saw my mom this week."

Paige had stabbed a grape on her fork and lifted it to her mouth, but when he'd said that, she lowered it. "You saw her? In person?"

He nodded. "My grandmother had texted me and said my mother had showed up at her house. When I got there she's all decked out in clothes I think she bought from your sister's store. She didn't look like the woman I'd remembered."

"You think she was at my sister's store?"

"She was. But it was a short and less than sweet visit. Basically I told her I wasn't interested in seeing her again."

Paige turned over her hand and linked their fingers. "You don't want to get to know her?"

"Oh, let me finish my story, and you decide what I should do."

Paige eased back in her chair and bit the grape off the fork.

"Remember that I told you there was a patron at the bar that set me off?" Paige nodded remembering the text he'd sent her. "Well, that was my mother."

"She went to the tap house?"

"She'd been in there a few times. The guys said she'd been in there asking about me."

"I can't believe she's been around and you didn't know."

"It gets better." Oliver picked up his fork and ate a strawberry. "To get her to leave, I told her I'd meet her for breakfast at Molly's and hear what she had to say. So Saturday morning, I met her. She's been married to some guy she met at a shelter when they'd cleaned up the area. Which is something they do when they're tired of people camping in the park."

"She was homeless."

"People choose to be homeless. I mean, not all of them, but some. My parents looked at it as a freedom, but the city sees it differently."

"I can't imagine."

"Anyway, she met this guy at the shelter who was doing community service for a DUI. They kept in touch, and eventually she married him."

"Wow."

"Yeah, wow." Oliver took another strawberry and ate it. "They've been married ten years, and here's the kicker. They have lived here for eight of those."

Paige set her fork down and reached for his hand. "She's been here for eight years and never reached out to you?"

"Ideal parent, huh?"

"Oliver, I don't know what to say."

"Well, now they're in financial trouble, and she wanted my help."

"Nice timing," Paige quipped.

"Right? Leave it to my own mother to show up when the shit has hit the fan for me."

"I can give you your money back."

His eyes narrowed at that. "Like hell you will. I told her that I had just invested in a new company and that I couldn't help her out. Even if that money was still in my account, I wouldn't help her."

"Where is your dad?"

"Dead."

Paige covered her mouth when a gasp escaped it. "I'm so sorry."

"Paige, I didn't know him any better than I knew her. Trust me, I don't need sympathy. When my grandfather died, that was devastating. This is just news."

"So she wants money. When you told her no, that was that?"

Oliver shook his head. "Of course not. She'd already been by the tap room by the time I stopped by there on Monday. But," he lifted his brows and smiled, "here's some positive news. So I stayed and worked with Jeff and Craig, and we closed out the drawer together. We all agreed on the total and I signed the sheet. It came back missing money."

"Someone is targeting you?"

"It appears to be the bookkeeper."

"That's good news, right?"

He chuckled. "Joel and Jeff are going to talk to them. But we're still losing money. If we can clear my name, that's one unfortunate thing off my plate."

Paige cupped his face in her hands. "It's all just bad timing. That's all."

"I hope so. I'd hate for you to finally have gotten involved with me and then for everything to go to shit."

"Luckily, I've known you long enough to know this isn't how it always goes for you. And I've been around the tap house since the beginning. I know just how much you've put into it and how much has come out of it—positively."

Oliver leaned in and pressed a kiss to her lips. "It's funny. I had finally thought things were going my way. I had you, I had a career I wanted, and there were ample opportunities for me."

"It's still like that," Paige promised kissing him again. "I'm still here, and I love you."

Oliver's phone buzzed in his pocket and he pulled it out and looked at it. "For heaven's sake."

"Who is it?"

"My mother."

Paige bit down on her lip. How was he supposed move on from everything going on if the woman didn't step aside like he'd asked her to do?

"What does she want?"

Oliver turned off his phone. "She has something to tell me. I can't imagine what more she has to tell me that we didn't discuss when she had a chance." He ran his hand over his beard. "I'm sorry. I seem to be a real downer today."

"No. We're in this together," she said, directing his attention back to her. "Listen, back to what you asked me before, about partners. I really feel as if we are partners. It's new. It's exciting. It's scary right now. But I want to be part of everything with you."

"Really?"

"Really. So what do you say, I'm going to get ready and head to the bank to get everything I need for tomorrow. Then, let's go for a hike."

"It's cold out, Paige."

She laughed. "Well, we'll wear coats and walk faster."

CHAPTER 37

Paige walked into the bank and over to Amy's desk. "Hello, Amy," she said as she sat down and the woman across from her lifted her head to see her.

"Hi, Paige. I was just getting ready to call you," she said, but Paige worried when Amy's brows had furrowed and she shuffled the papers on her desk.

"Oh, what did you need?"

"It's about that deposit you made last week. It appears that they weren't able to secure those funds, and they didn't deposit."

Paige felt a tightening in her chest. "I'm sorry. The funds didn't deposit?"

"No."

"So it's not in my account?"

"No."

Paige's hands began to tremble. "Why wouldn't it have gone through?"

Amy folded her hands on top of her desk. "There are many reasons, but more than likely, it means that the account the check was drawn on didn't have enough money in it."

"The check bounced."

"Probably so. I don't have a lot of information other than the deposit didn't go through. You'll have to follow up with the issuer of the check."

"Right."

"Is everything okay?"

Paige batted her eyes. "I'm not sure. But thank you. I'll be in touch."

On wobbly legs, Paige stood and managed to get herself out of the bank and to her car before tears began to stream down her cheeks.

How had he possibly written her a check that wasn't any good? Why would Oliver have done that?

Now what was she supposed to do? She had plenty of people offer to give her the money, but she'd taken his money, and now she had nothing to give Pricilla to buy the business. Everything she'd been planning for was officially on hold.

Paige wiped the tears from her face and started the car. As she backed out of the parking space and began to drive, she realized she wasn't even sure where she was going to go. Did Oliver know what he'd done to her dreams? Why had he offered her the money if he didn't even have it? The more she thought about it, the more she had to wonder if that was why the money had started to go missing at the tap house. God, had he taken it because he was in some kind of trouble?

No. She loved the man and didn't think he would steal and lie. Then again, how well did she know him? Sure, she'd known him now for years, and they were friends, but they'd never discussed the many things they had in the past month. Even her father had once pulled the wool over his wife's eyes and the woman he was dating. Shit!

She slammed on her brakes at the light, narrowly missing the car in front of her. Paige needed to clear her mind and secure the funds for the purchase of the business. Turning at the next light, she headed toward Max's.

. . .

THE MOMENT MAX opened the front door, Paige fell into his arms and sobbed.

"Whoa. Hey, what's wrong? What happened? Did someone hurt you?" Max managed as he pulled her into the house and closed the door. "Take a breath, Paige."

Paige wiped the tears that ran down her cheeks. "I think he's in trouble. I think something is wrong, and Oliver is in trouble."

"C'mon. Let's sit down."

Max took her by the arm and led her to the kitchen of the house his wife had grown up in, and they were in the process of remodeling. The kitchen looked like a construction site, but no doubt Max would make it look perfect.

"Sit down," he instructed as he walked to the refrigerator and pulled out two bottles of water. "Drink and get calm. Then tell me what happened."

Paige twisted the top from the bottle and sipped the water as she tried to gather her thoughts.

"You know that money had been missing from the tap house, from his shifts?" she asked to gauge what he knew.

"Yes. That was mentioned to me. But Joel also said he didn't really think he did it."

"Well, no, I didn't think so either. I think it's a bookkeeping error. But now his mom is in town and she's begging him for money. And, I just went to the bank to get the cashier's check to take to the closing tomorrow, and the money he gave me didn't clear the bank. I don't have money to buy the company now," she said sobbing again.

"Paige, let's break this down. His mom needs money?"

"He hasn't seen his mother since he was eight. And now she's showing up and wanting him to lend her money."

"That's heavy."

"Right? He told her no and to leave him alone, but she keeps coming back."

"Okay. And the bookkeeping error?"

Paige shook her head. "I think someone is stealing it to make it look like Oliver."

"One of the partners?"

She winced. "I don't think so. Which one of them would do that?"

"Okay, so someone on the outside that knows them all and maybe has something against Oliver."

Paige nodded. "Yes, or so I hope. What if he's in some kind of trouble?"

"Then I guess you'd better decide how you're going to handle that. How involved are you?"

"Max, I love him."

"You're sure?"

She narrowed her eyes on him. "Do you love Meghann?" She saw him shift in his seat. "Of course you do. I do, I love him. We've been attracted for a long time, and now, well now it's love."

"Okay, okay," he ran his hand over the stubble on his chin. "Have you talked to him?"

"Not yet. I just drove here. I didn't know where else to go."

"Funny, I didn't think I'd be your first choice."

Paige laughed. He was the least likely to give her solid relationship advice, but it was where she'd ended up.

"I think you need to talk to him first. Maybe he has an answer. Maybe he doesn't even know what happened."

She hadn't even thought of that. "Okay. I'll do that."

"Let me get my keys," Max said standing from his seat.

"Why? Where are you going?"

"You're going to meet me at the bank. We need to get you the funds for that business you're opening. Remember, I'm coming to start renovation next week."

Paige stood and hugged her brother. "You're still going to do that for me?"

"I have the means, and since I sold my company, I have the time. Paige, I believe in you. I think Oliver does too. But I think he's in trouble and we need to help him."

Her siblings had never let her down. What would she do without them?

CHAPTER 38

The frantic phone call Oliver had received from his grandmother had him racing to the pharmacy where she was waiting for him.

"I need my prescriptions, but my debit card won't go through. When I called them, because the lady said I could use their phone, they said I didn't have any money in my account. I asked them for specific totals, and they said that was the specific total."

Oliver put his arm around his grandmother, her body shaking as she sat in the chair in the pharmacy.

"When did you check your balance last?"

"Three days ago when my check was supposed to be deposited. I always make sure it's in the bank and I had plenty of money in there. I keep that account well padded."

He knew she did. She never wanted to be without, especially after his grandfather had died.

"We'll get this figured out," he said holding his grandmother to him.

Who would mess with a woman on a fixed income? What reward was there in that, he wondered, and then his heart sank in his chest.

The one person who needed money, and had come looking for it, would be the most likely to specifically target the woman he held. Damnit, he should have seen that coming.

Oliver paid for the medication with the cash he had in his pocket and saw his grandmother back home. When he knew she was settled, he'd start investigating what had happened. His mother could mess with him, but not his grandmother. That was off limits.

AN HOUR later he pulled up to his house and Paige paced on his front porch. Worry shrouded her face, and he wondered what else the day could bring.

Quickly, Oliver killed the engine and stepped out of the car. As soon as he did, Paige started toward him.

"If you didn't want me to have it, you shouldn't have given it to me. Or if you couldn't afford to give it to me, you just shouldn't have."

The words came so quickly they jumbled in his brain.

Oliver took hold of her shoulders and she flinched, so he dropped his hands. "I have no idea what you're saying," he admitted.

Paige's eyes welled with tears. "Why did you even bother?"

"Bother with what?"

"To give me the check if you knew you didn't have the money?"

He narrowed his eyes on her. "I do have it. What are you trying to tell me?" He shook his head. "No. Wait. Let's go inside. I have a feeling I'm going to want to be sitting down for this."

They walked up the front steps and Oliver opened the door. Paige went inside and continued her pacing in the living room.

"Let's make some tea," he offered, expecting some push back, but Paige followed him into the kitchen.

She sat down at the little table and bit at her fingernails while

Oliver started the kettle. Once it was on the burner, he turned and leaned against the counter.

"Okay, let's try this again," he said calmly.

Paige looked up at him. "I didn't mean to come across like that. I'd worked it up in my head that there had to be some kind of mistake, or I don't know, a payment you didn't know about went through. I didn't mean to jump you like that. Max told me to talk to you, not to accuse you."

Oliver nodded slowly. "Let's put some things in order. The money I gave you, it's not in your account?"

Paige batted her eyes and took a breath. "No. The funds never went through."

"And you've already talked to Max about this?"

"I had to talk to someone, and I went to him. And he also gave me the money for the business."

Oliver nodded again taking in all the information, only now his head spun and he needed to sit down.

Paige took his hand. "Are you in some kind of trouble?"

That made him chuckle. "I wasn't, but now I'm not so sure." Oliver ran his free hand over his beard. "I just came from the pharmacy where my grandmother was in hysterics because her debit card didn't work. They let her call the bank, and they told her she didn't have any money. My grandmother always has a nest egg."

Paige retracted her hand and covered her mouth. "Someone is targeting you. From the tap house accounts, to your accounts, to your grandmother's accounts. Why?"

Oliver ran his tongue against the inside of his cheek. "Only one person would target me and my grandmother. I should have seen this coming when she wrote me that first letter."

"Your mother?"

"Yeah, my mother. How else would they get into my grandmother's account?"

"How could anyone do that to their child or their mother?"

Oliver stood and paced the kitchen. "This is the kind of shit that keeps me up at night. I mean worrying about what kind of person she was, they were. They never came for me. They didn't provide for me. And now, all these years later, she steals from me. Is that genetic? Will I treat someone like that? Will there be a day when you walk into the bay and don't come back, and I don't even care?"

Her eyes had gone wide. "Is that what happened to your father?"

Oliver threw his hands up. "I don't know. What I'm saying is, will I hurt the people I love and who trust me because it's in my DNA? Why the hell would anyone want that?"

The tears that had pooled in Paige's eyes fell, and it crushed him, but he didn't move to her. Now not only was someone stealing from him, but he was second guessing everything he thought he knew. Paige deserved better. His partners deserved better.

Oliver ran his hand over his hair. "Maybe you should go. You have a lot to do this week, and it looks like I have some to do as well."

"You're just going to dismiss me? You're not the only one hurt in this. Something has to be done."

"I'll take care of it. No one needs my drama in their lives. You all were doing fine before."

Paige stood. "So were you. I love you. Don't push me away."

Oliver shook his head. "I'm not sure I'm capable of love, Paige, so don't waste it on me."

Now her lip trembled as tears continued down her cheeks. She took a breath to say something else, but she never did. Instead she hurried to the door and slammed it on her way out.

CHAPTER 39

Oliver's blood pulsed in his veins. The more he thought about what was happening, the angrier he got.

With his laptop open, he searched his bank accounts. Sure enough, the day after he'd left the check for Paige, money had been pulled from his account.

Perhaps that was his fault after all. Oliver didn't thrive on money, so checking to see where it was every day wasn't part of his routine. He loved his work. He loved working out in his garage. The items in his house were for necessity only, so there was never need to worry about anything.

He slammed down the top to the laptop and thought about the letter his mother had written him the month before. Like he'd told Paige, that should have been his first clue that things were going to go badly. Damnit!

Looking down at the notebook next to him, he looked at the amounts and dates where he'd noticed money leaving his account. And, because it was his shifts that were targeted at the tap house, there was no reason to think that his mother hadn't somehow finagled herself into that account too. Was she out for vengeance?

She'd messed with him, his business, his grandmother, and now it had affected the woman he loved. Where would it end?

~

CRAIG NARROWED his eyes at Oliver as he walked through the back door and headed for the office where Joel and Jeff sat.

"What's missing now?" he asked as he shut the door behind him and both sets of eyes wearily looked up at him.

"What are you doing here?"

"I own part of this company, and don't you dare talk to me like that," he said angrily as his pulse throbbed. "Someone is messing with us and they started with me."

Oliver paced the office as Craig pushed through the door and headed right to him.

"My car payment bounced. My mortgage didn't get paid. And my debit card didn't work at the pump this morning," he said as he shoved Oliver up against the wall.

Jeff swiftly moved between them as Joel came around the desk and pulled Craig from Oliver.

"Stop it!" Joel shouted. "Why in the hell would he come in here if he robbed us blind?" he said as he pushed Craig back. "God, we all need to calm down and keep our heads about us."

Joel wiped the back of his hand across his forehead and sat back down behind the desk.

Oliver raked his fingers through his hair, his eyes steady on Craig. "So now we've all been hit."

"Looks like it. All except Jeff who gets a paper check instead of direct deposit," Joel said.

All eyes shifted in Jeff's direction. "And don't go accusing me. I have more mouths to feed than anyone."

Oliver put his hands on the back of the chair that faced the desk. "My grandmother's account was hit. My personal account too. And," he let out a sigh, "the check I wrote Paige for the well-ness center bounced."

Joel nodded. "I heard."

"Family gossip travels fast," Oliver quipped.

"You have no idea." Joel pulled up another site which Oliver recognized as the bookkeepers that Joel and Jeff had chosen for the company. "I hate that I have to go and accuse someone of wrongdoing, but it all leads here."

"Oh, I think you all got really good at the accusing," Oliver spat out the words and noticed that Craig flinched as if he were going to go after him again, but then backed down.

"And for that I'm truly sorry," Joel said.

"So am I," Jeff agreed.

But nothing came from Craig.

Oliver paced a circle in the room and then headed for the door. "Before you go breaking ties with a business associates and accusing them of fraud, I have a phone call to make."

Craig moved toward him now. "To your lawyer?"

"Pull your head out of your ass," Oliver growled. "We're all in this."

Jeff stepped forward, and Oliver recognized the defensive move to keep Craig from attacking again. "Who are you calling?"

"My mother."

Thursday morning, Paige sat in the office of Pricilla's lawyer and waited for them to walk through the door. The folder of paperwork she held in her hands shook. Buying the business might have been a mistake, she decided. Just as professing her love to Oliver had been.

What had she been thinking? He'd been a mystery to her for years, and that had been some of his appeal. Though, when she'd learned all about his life, she had to admit to herself it had made her love him even more.

When the door opened, Pricilla and man in a suit walked through the door. Paige stood, knocking the folder to the ground.

She bent to pick it up and laughed. "I'm nervous I guess," she admitted.

Pricilla, smelling of essential oils touched her arm. "We all are. Oh, I'll be happy to have free time, but it's nerve wracking. But I know you'll take my little business and do great things with it. You've always had a mind for business and I know your vision. This is a blessing."

Paige smiled, but her mind spun thinking of everything that had happened to get to that point.

The lawyer introduced himself and Paige shook his hand before they all sat down.

Papers were discussed and signed, and Paige thought she just might be sick the moment she handed over the check that Max had secured for her.

"It looks like everything is in order," the lawyer said. "I can leave you two for a few moments to finish any personal business."

Pricilla thanked him, and they both watched as he left the room.

"You look like you might pass out, darling. Isn't this what you wanted?"

Paige bit down on her lip. "Yes. It is. I'll be okay."

Pricilla reached for her hand and patted it. "By the way, love looks good on you."

"I beg your pardon?"

"That man that comes to your classes, your brother-in-law's business partner. I know that there has been an energy shift between the two of you. The room buzzes when he walks into it."

"It does?"

Pricilla nodded. "But I feel as if there is some distress there now."

She sure was observant. "A little. But it'll all work itself out."

"Well, don't give up." Pricilla stood and draped her bag across her. "If something isn't worked at or for, what's it worth?"

She gave Paige a small wave and let herself out of the office.

Paige rested back in the chair and took a deep breath. Was it worth working for? Yes, of course it was.

CHAPTER 40

Oliver had been calling the number his mother left for him for two days, and there hadn't been an answer. Sure, now when he needed her, she was nowhere—then again, that was the norm.

He'd heard from Joel that the bookkeeper had come for the deposits and the bookwork. Joel had told him under the circumstances, they were going to hold on to the cash deposit and paperwork. That hadn't sat well with the man, and Joel thought they might be looking for a new bookkeeper for the future.

Oliver had spent the previous night with his grandmother, sorting through her expenses and trying to make arrangements until they could secure funds again. He felt helpless. He couldn't even loan her the money. Any assets he did retain were locked up and the penalty, though worth it to gain access to the money, would outweigh making a few phone calls. But if it came to it, Monday morning, he'd liquidate.

"Oliver, don't you fret. I'll open a new bank account on Monday, and I'll have my checks deposited there. In a month, things will be back to normal. And Thursday is Thanksgiving, and you'll be here. I have plenty of stuff in the freezer to make dinner, even if it's not traditional," she'd said.

He chuckled. There had been the difference between his grandmother and his mother, his grandmother always saw the silver lining.

She was optimistic, and he appreciated that about her, but what if something happened to her before the next check came in? Oliver tried to keep the worry off of his face, but he was sure she'd seen right through it.

Blane moved around Oliver's feet, he supposed it was to remind him that he was still there. Of course, when he bent to pick him up, Blane moved on as if he had other plans.

Oliver picked up his phone to call his mother one more time, only this time his phone rang in his hand.

He studied the number. It was local, but he didn't recognize it. Surely collectors were going to start calling and looking for payment since any checks he'd sent out were going to bounce.

The option was to let it go to voice mail, or he could answer and handle the situation. As it rang again, he connected the call.

"Hello."

"Hi, I'm looking for an Ollie Ferguson," the woman on the other end said.

Oliver couldn't help but laugh. "I'm sorry. I think you have the wrong number."

"I might have the name wrong," the woman admitted. "It's a contact in a phone that belongs to a Ms. Daisy Ferguson."

Oliver swallowed hard. He didn't even know his mother's last name. "Daisy is my mother's name. She does call me Ollie."

"We might be making progress then," the woman said. "The contact for Ollie says son."

"And you are?"

"I'm Janet Pomeroy. I'm a nurse at Saint Paul's."

The blood drained from Oliver's head and he closed his eyes. "My mother is there?"

"Yes. She's in our care. Would you be able to come down?"

Oliver ran his hand down his beard, and then again. "Is she okay?"

"She's stable. The doctors would like to discuss it with you in person."

"I'll be right down."

OLIVER COULDN'T REMEMBER a stop light or sign on his way to the hospital. It was possible he'd blown through all of them.

The nurse had told him they'd be moving his mother from emergency to an intermediate care unit, but he didn't understand any of it. All he could do was try to keep it from making his mind fuzzy.

The volunteer at the front desk directed him to the floor his mother was on, and another volunteer at a desk directed him to a waiting area where someone would come to talk to him.

It had been a long time since he'd been so conflicted with emotions. He'd pushed his mother away, and he hadn't wanted to see her, but never had he wanted something bad to happen to her. Had it been self-inflicted? Had she been in an accident?

His phone buzzed in his hand and he looked down to see the text from Paige.

Let's talk.

He couldn't even wrap his head around that right now. If she truly loved him, she'd wait for a reply.

A woman in a white coat walked over to him. "Are you Oliver?"

He stood. "Oliver Westcott. I'm Daisy Ferguson's son." The name sounded foreign as he said it.

"Let's sit," the woman said as she sat in the chair directly across from him. "I'm Doctor Price. I'm taking care of your mother."

"I don't know why she's here. No one has told me anything."

Doctor Price crossed her legs and rested her hands on her knee. "Your mother was found in an alley. She had been severely beaten, and we believe left for dead."

Oliver pressed his fingers to his eyes. The first thought that came to mind was how much he wished Paige was there with him to take in all of this information.

"Do you know anything about it?"

Oliver lowered his hands and shook his head. "I haven't seen my mother for twenty-three years. She wrote me a letter a month ago, and showed up last week looking for money."

"When we pulled her record, it looks like maybe she had some problems a few years back with drugs."

He nodded. "I would assume so. But she's married now, or that's what she told me. When they called to say she was here, it was the first time I'd heard the Ferguson name."

"Mason Ferguson comes up as her husband, but we haven't been able to get hold of him."

Why did that name sound familiar? Oliver decided it was common enough.

"I don't know him."

Doctor Price rested a hand atop his. "Would you like to see her?"

He wasn't sure. Was that wrong?

No, he needed to see her. Since she'd sent that letter, his life had been nothing but a mess. He needed to see her in case it was his very last time.

CHAPTER 41

Doctor Price escorted Oliver to the room where they had his mother. There were windows so she could be monitored, and a nurse stood over her as they entered. As she turned to leave, she said, "She's awake."

Doctor Price approached the bed and Oliver was surprised just how badly he wanted to run the other direction.

"Daisy, your son is here. Do you want to see him?"

He heard his mother's weak voice. "Yes."

Doctor Price turned to him. "Someone will be just outside to monitor her. If you need anything, just let them know."

As she walked past him, he turned to see his mother in the bed. After twenty-three years she had been unrecognizable to him, but now even that image had been shattered.

Her blonde hair was matted with blood, though it looked as though an attempt had been made to clean it up. Both of her eyes were swollen nearly shut, and her cheek was twice its normal size. Her lips were cut and bruised, and he was very sure there were fingerprints bruised into her neck.

Was he supposed to cry, because instead he felt as if he might vomit.

"Ollie," her voice was just a whisper and he saw her fingers twitch as if she were trying to reach for him.

"I'm here," he said as he sucked in a breath and as much courage as he could muster.

Oliver took the seat next to the bed and covered his mother's hand with his. "I'm here," he said again.

She'd gone silent and he wondered if those few words she'd spoken had already exhausted her. A few minutes later she stirred and rolled her head as if she could see him, though he wasn't sure she could.

"I survived." The words were strained and now he could feel the tears welling in his eyes.

"You're going to be okay. They're going to take care of you."

Again, she'd gone silent and it was then Oliver noticed the police officer walking the floor outside the room. Were they there to protect his mother or accuse him of leaving her like this?

"Mason," she whispered and Oliver had to focus to understand.

"Mason. Mason Ferguson is your husband. Right?"

His mother's fingers twitched under his and he took that as her answer.

"I can find him. I'll let him know you're here."

This time her fingers didn't twitch and she moaned instead.

"You don't want me to find him?"

She moved her fingers.

"Mom, did Mason do this to you?"

Her fingers moved again.

THEY HAD GIVEN his mother something for the pain and he'd had a long conversation with the police officer before he'd left.

Oliver sat in his car at a stop light and rubbed his eyes. The officer told him they'd had many domestic disturbance calls to his mother's house, but she always claimed that nothing had happened.

Had she moved to town to get away from the monster she'd married, or had she thought he'd be someone different here? Was he the reason it had taken her eight years of living within miles of Oliver for her to finally contact him?

Now guilt squeezed in his chest. He didn't have answers.

Pulling up behind the tap house, Oliver turned off his engine and stepped out onto the gravel.

"Are you not getting your texts or are you ignoring me?" Paige's voice cut through the drama that was playing over and over in his head.

Oliver turned to see her walking toward him from the back door of Kennedy's store. As usual, there were others watching from the window in Kennedy's break room.

"Paige, listen—"

"No, you listen," she interrupted. "I don't know what has happened to you in the past week, but I'm very afraid for you. Are you in trouble?"

"There is just so much to process, I don't know where to begin."

"Begin with are you in trouble?"

"No."

Paige stepped closer to him. "Okay. A lot of people around me are very mad."

"As they should be. But I have other issues now."

"Your mother?"

"Yeah," he said and he felt the tears sting his eyes, but he batted them away. "Do you have some time to come inside? I need to sit down and process some things."

Paige held her hand out and took his. "You might have dismissed me the other day, but I do love you, Oliver. If that helps you get through this, I'm grateful. If it doesn't, I'd understand."

Oliver pulled her to him and wrapped his arms around her.

"It's going to help." He pressed a kiss to her lips. "Did you get your yoga studio?"

Paige laughed as she placed a hand on his cheek. "Yes. Max is already ripping stuff up."

"I can't wait to see it."

HAND IN HAND they walked through the back door of the tap house, and Paige felt the icy stare of Oliver's partners as they walked in and went directly to the office.

Oliver moved behind the desk and Paige moved to the corner of the room as Joel walked in and closed the door behind him.

"Did you get a hold of your mom?" Joel asked and Oliver looked up from the keyboard.

"Well, sort of. She found me. Or they found me," he said shaking his head as he set his hands flat on the desk.

"That doesn't make any sense," Joel said.

"Nothing in the past week has made any sense. Why does the name Mason Ferguson sound familiar to me?"

Joel cleared his throat. "Mason Ferguson?"

"Yeah. I can't place the name."

"Dude, he's the bookkeeper."

CHAPTER 42

Oliver felt as if he'd been punched in the gut.

Paige skirted the desk. "You just went white. Are you okay?"

"No," he said shaking his head. "No, I'm not okay."

Joel moved to the desk, placing his hands atop it, he leaned in. "What do you have to do with Mason Ferguson?"

Oliver wasn't going to react to the insinuating tone that had lowered Joel's voice. Everything in that moment had come to light, and the only thing he had to do with Mason Ferguson was to find him.

"Mason Ferguson is my mother's husband."

Joel's eyes went wide and Oliver stood, holding his hand off to ward off anything that might be said.

"I found this out about an hour ago when I was at the hospital where they have my mother." He watched two sets of eyes soften. "They found her in an alley. She'd been beaten and left for dead. When they called me, they called looking for Ollie Ferguson."

Joel pinched the bridge of his nose. "No one calls you Ollie."

"Right. I was in her phone as Ollie and it had son with it. They pieced together the Ferguson because of her husband's name. It appears they've had many calls to their house for domestic disputes, but then my mother always changes her story."

"They think Mason did that to your mom?"

Oliver nodded. "She couldn't talk much, but she was trying to tell me that Mason had done that to her. And now, with this, it double fits."

Jeff opened the door and slid into the room, closing it behind him. "What's going on?"

"Super sleuth, P.I. shit," Joel said as he sat down in the chair next to him. "Oliver's mom is in the hospital. Someone beat her and dumped her in an alley."

Even Jeff's eyes went sympathetic. "Man, I'm sorry."

"Me too." Oliver ran his hand over his hair. "Where did you guys find Mason Ferguson?"

Jeff exchanged glances with Oliver and Joel. "We got referrals. He wasn't our original guy. It seems like he just came along and was assigned to us. Do we think Mason is the one that is messing with the money? I mean I know we considered it. And when he came for the deposit and the book work he got a little testy when we said we were going to hold on to it."

Oliver nodded. "That makes sense. It also makes sense why it was my shifts that were targeted. My checking account is wiped out and so was my grandmother's. I know they hit you guys too."

"They?" Jeff asked.

Oliver shrugged. "I have to assume my mother was in on this." He blew out a breath. "Then again, maybe not. Craig said she'd come in on Saturday after I had breakfast with her and left her number. She told him she wanted me to call her."

"You didn't?" Joel asked.

"Not until yesterday, and she didn't take my calls." And now he knew why and it made him sick again.

Paige rested her hand on his shoulder. "Do you think she was trying to warn you?"

Oliver lifted his eyes to her. "I don't know. I didn't give her a chance. She did tell me that they were struggling. I told her I wouldn't help her, but it didn't seem as if she were there to tell me her husband was stealing from me."

Jeff pulled his phone from his pocket. "You've talked to the police?"

Oliver pulled the card from his pocket that the officer at the hospital had given him. "This was the officer assigned to my mother."

Jeff nodded. "I think we need to give him a call."

Upon Paige's suggestion, Oliver headed back to the hospital to see his mother.

He had decided against telling his grandmother about the situation, for now. She'd have to be told, but Oliver just wasn't ready to bring her that kind of news.

There was still a police officer stationed outside his mother's room. Oliver made sure to introduce himself before walking into her room.

His mother was resting, and he stood near the door to watch her for a moment.

The swelling around her eyes had gone down, but the bruises were darker. Oliver could see her arms fully now, and they too were covered in cuts and bruises. How could someone do that to another person, he wondered.

"Ollie," he heard the whisper that had come from his mother.

Walking toward her, he felt his limbs grow heavy. He noticed her fingers twitching, and he reached for her hand.

"I wanted to check on you," he said looking down at her. "Your swelling has gone down."

The corner of her mouth curled a bit, as if she were trying to smile. "You're here," she whispered.

"Yeah, I'm here."

There wasn't anything she could tell him, yet. He knew that his being there was going to help her heal. So, holding his mother's hand, he sat in the chair next to her bed.

CHAPTER 43

In a matter of days, Max had completely torn apart the wellness center to convert it into Paige's dream yoga studio.

Walls were patched, the wood floor had been sanded, and that ugly paneling in the entryway had been taken down. She'd had to postpone classes until after Thanksgiving, but it was worth it. Luckily, her students were equally as excited.

Paige was no stranger to early Saturday mornings, and the massage therapist she was interviewing wasn't either. It made for a nice time to talk over a cup of tea in the break room that Max had created from an old office space.

It had taken less than thirty minutes to decide that Pepper, the massage therapist, was the right person to fill the space at the studio, but they had gotten along so well, it was an hour before she'd stood to leave.

"I'm anxious to get started," Pepper said. "I really like your vision."

Paige smiled as she held her hand out to her. "I'm anxious too. I've wanted to build a studio like this for a long time."

"It's going to be epic."

As Pepper turned to leave, the front door opened and Oliver walked in. His eyes were dark and his hair wore tunnels where his fingers had raked through multiple times.

"I'll text you when Max gets the room put together and we can discuss colors and such," Paige said with the smile forced to her lips but aware of how rough Oliver looked.

"I'll talk to you then." Pepper shook Paige's hand and gave Oliver a friendly smile as she walked out the door.

As soon as Pepper had walked out of view, Paige moved to Oliver and wrapped her arms around him. "You look horrible. Tell me everything is okay."

His arms came around her and he buried his face against her neck.

Paige held him as he just breathed.

"Oliver, you're scaring me."

He pressed a kiss against her neck before easing back and rested his forehead. "I've sat with her all night," he said, his voice low. "She's going to be okay, but the road is going to be long."

"And you're going to see her through it, aren't you?"

Oliver let out a breath. "I have a lot to think about. Until then, yeah, I'll see her though this. Of course, I have to tell my grandmother."

"She doesn't know yet?"

"I didn't want to pile it all on her."

"You need some sleep."

Oliver stepped back. "I do. I need to go home and check on Blane."

"Give me a moment and I'll go with you. I think you should have someone drive. Seriously, you look horrible."

Oliver chuckled. "I'll wait for you."

Paige gathered her bag and turned off the lights. Max would be there soon to start working. She pulled the keys from her pocket, and she and Oliver stepped out the door. As Paige turned to lock the door, the ground beneath their feet, and the walls in front of them shook as an explosion blew the windows out of the tap house.

Paige and Oliver stumbled backward as the world around them rumbled, and a man plowed toward them as he ran from between the tap house and Kennedy's store. He was looking over his shoulder at the smoke that now billowed from the tap house and ran right into them, knocking all three of them to the ground.

Oliver fell back and the man on top of him, while Paige fell forward, her face hitting the pavement.

The man scrambled to get his feet under him, but Oliver maneuvered himself on top of him and his eyes went wide when he looked at the man, now bloodied from the explosion.

"Shit. Shit!" Oliver yelled as he turned and looked at Paige. "Call 9-1-1 and go make sure there wasn't anyone there yet. Hurry!"

As Paige got to her feet and ran down the street, Oliver pinned the man under him with his hands on his shoulders. A month ago he knew the man as the bookkeeper who came to get the paperwork and the deposit, but now he was the man who was single-handedly ruining his life. The man who had stolen from him, his friends, and his family—and had tried to kill his mother. And now the man had a name—Mason Ferguson.

"Will you not be happy until you've killed everyone I love?" Oliver pressed his hands down on the man who squirmed beneath him.

"I'll kill you. Get off of me!" The man hollered under him, but Oliver didn't ease up.

"You tried to kill my mother."

"You couldn't care less," the man beneath him spat out the words as he struggled to free himself. "She's lived near you and you didn't even know it. She lived on the streets, you lived this cozy life. People like you deserve what you get. You're a piece of shit, son," Mason growled as he pulled one arm free and grabbed the front of Oliver's shirt.

A moment later, Oliver felt a hand on his shoulder pulling him off of the man. As Oliver landed on his ass, he saw Craig and Joel jump on the man as he tried to get to his feet. Craig raised his fist and buried in Mason's gut before landing another punch across his jaw.

Paige ran back down the walk and fell next to Oliver as two police cars pulled up next to them and fire trucks, with sirens blaring, pulled up to the tap house.

Oliver shifted to the look at the smoke rising from the tap house, and then at Paige, whose face was split and bloody.

"You're okay?" he asked.

"I'm fine. I'm fine," she wept. "Look at you."

Oliver looked down to see that his shirt was ripped and he, too, had blood on him.

A hand extended toward him, and Craig helped him to his feet. Joel helped Paige up and the four of them walked toward the tap house as Jeff pulled up behind them and jumped from his truck.

He stood with them in the middle of the street as they all looked at the building they'd worked so hard to refurbish. Oliver, with his arm around Paige's shoulders, pulled her closer to him and placed a kiss to the top of her head.

As he looked at the faces of his partners, he saw in their eyes what he felt in his heart. They would rebuild. They were resilient.

CHAPTER 44

Oliver stood with Jeff, Joel, and Craig on the sidewalk outside Kingsley Tap House looking in through broken windows.

Jeff let out a long breath. "This is a kick in the balls."

Joel put his hand on his brother's shoulder. "I never liked the layout," he said smiling. "I think the bar needed to be longer."

That had caused them all to chuckle. Craig tucked his hands into the pockets of his coat. "We need a big, mirrored wall with the logo etched in it."

Oliver nudged Craig. "That's only because you like to look at yourself all day."

"Why wouldn't I?"

They laughed, but then it was somber again.

Jeff pulled on a pair of gloves. "He threw something through the window. Some homemade bomb of some sort."

Oliver crossed his arms in front of him to attempt to warm himself up. "I find it interesting that he didn't do this while we had people in there. I'm grateful," he said, "don't get me wrong. But after seeing what he did to my mother, humanity means nothing to him."

Joel wrapped an arm around Oliver's shoulder. "Paige is okay?"

"She's scuffed up, but she's fine."

"We have insurance. We'll rebuild."

"Damn straight we will. Max will be done with Paige's by next week. We can drag him into this."

Joel nodded. "He'd be invaluable."

Oliver moved to face his partners. "I don't know how I can ever make this up to all of you."

Joel stepped toward him. "What exactly do you have to make up for?"

"This happened because he was married to my mother. There was some vendetta he was taking out on us by stealing from us— from me. And now everything we worked so hard for is ash."

Jeff shook his head. "Joel and I hired the company and did business with the man. Equal involvement."

"You said he was assigned to us."

"Yep, and we didn't check him out. So if he actually got the job to screw you over, well, then he got something out of it. But we're all still here, and we're not going anywhere. In less than six months, we'll be back in business."

Oliver wouldn't cry in front of his friends, but it took everything he had to push back the tears. "You don't hold this against me?"

Now Craig moved toward him. "I was kind of an ass about this before. I owe you an apology. And, no, I don't hold this against you." He held out his hand and Oliver shook it. "By the way, how's your mom?"

Now the tears Oliver tried to hide welled in his eyes. "She's stable. They moved her into another room and want to keep her for a few more days. My grandmother is with her right now."

Joel smiled. "That says a lot."

"It does. It says my grandmother is an amazingly forgiving person."

"And you?"

"I'll have to learn," Oliver admitted.

The pink door to Kennedy's store opened and she stepped out. "We have some sandwiches and chips. My mother-in-law made some brownies, and the bakery has sent over some cookies. Why don't you boys come in from the cold?"

Oliver and his partners walked into the boutique. Each of their eyes went wide when they saw the damage inside of Kennedy's store. It wasn't anything that couldn't be cleaned up in a matter of days, but seeing the damage squeezed at his heart.

There was a table set up with food and drinks. A few fire-fighters that were still working on the tap room had gathered for the sandwiches offered. Kennedy, Hillary, Meghann, and Joel's mother moved about filling glasses and making plates. Chase carried his daughter on his hip and held the hand of his niece getting them settled to have some food.

Oliver moved to Paige and pressed a kiss to Paige's lips. "This is very nice of you all to set this up."

"A lot goes into putting out a fire."

He lifted his hand to her face, careful not touch the scratches that now were bruised. "I'm so sorry this happened to you."

"It could have happened for any reason, by anyone. I'm okay. We're all okay."

Oliver looked around the store. "Did she lose a lot in here?"

Paige shook her head. "It'll be easily cleaned up and the few things replaced. Don't worry about her."

"I always will."

Paige rested her head on his shoulder. "What are you guys going to do?"

"We'll rebuild. There is no question there."

"I figured. You know, I've seen restaurants and businesses that have gone through the same thing put up a tent and run from under it."

Oliver kissed the top of her head now. "You're a genius, sweetheart. I'll have to talk to them about that."

"In time." Now she reached her hand to his scuffed up cheek. "We should have had you checked out." She looked at his arms and his bruised hand. "Are you sure nothing is broken?"

"Just my heart, but it'll mend."

Paige wrapped her arms around him. "I love you. I'm all yours between classes. I'll help you rebuild."

"With help like that, we'll be back up and running in no time."

She eased back to look up at him. "You know each and every Devereaux will be there to help you too."

"I know. We're lucky to have you all." Oliver took her hands. "I should head to the hospital and check in on my mother and grandmother."

"Do you think you'll reconcile?"

"We'll see what happens. Or, we'll see if my grandmother makes me."

Paige laughed. "I'll go with you if you'd like."

Her dark eyes sparkled as she looked up at him. "I would like that."

CHAPTER 45

Hand in hand, Oliver and Paige walked down the hall in the hospital to the room where they had moved his mother. Oliver smiled when he saw her. Though the cuts and bruises were dark and purple, her eyes were open, and the corner of her mouth curled when she saw him.

His grandmother stood and moved to him, kissing him on the cheek.

"Paige, let's go get some coffee," she said taking hold of Paige's arm and leading her away from the room.

Oliver walked to the side of his mother's bed and she moved her hand for him to hold hers.

"You look better."

She nodded slightly. "She's stayed with me," she whispered, obvious that her throat still hurt.

"She's a very forgiving woman."

"Are you a forgiving man?"

Oliver let out a breath. "I'm working on it."

His mother's fingers gripped his hand tighter. "She told me what Mason did."

With his free hand, Oliver ran it over his beard. "We'll rebuild.

But the important part is they have him in custody. He's been charged with what he did to you, to me, to Grandma, my partners, and what he did to our business. It'll be a long time before we have to worry about him."

He saw the tears welling in his mother's eyes and he moved closer to her.

"What you need to do is get better. You need to heal and then we can talk about forgiving and moving on, okay?"

His mother nodded slightly.

Paige and his grandmother walked back into the room, each carrying a cup of coffee.

Oliver held his hand out to Paige, and when she took it, he pulled her next to him. "Mom, this is Paige Devereaux."

She smiled more fully now, though he could see that it hurt her to do so. "I met you at the pink store," she said softly.

"My sister Kennedy's store."

"Yes."

Oliver gave Paige's hand a squeeze. "It's nice to meet you."

His mother studied them. "You're a nice couple."

THEY'D STAYED at the hospital for an hour and then he'd taken Paige back to her studio and driven his grandmother home.

Without discussion, he followed her into the kitchen where she put her tea kettle on the stove.

It had been a long time since he'd seen such worry and exhaustion on his grandmother's face. He watched as she tied on an apron, pulled down the mugs and the box of teas. She set them on the table and retrieved her cookie jar.

"I baked the other night when I was worked up," she said lifting the lid. "No limit tonight." She winked at Oliver, who once had a very bad cookie habit.

When the kettle whistled, she carried it to the table and

poured water into each of their mugs before returning it to the stove. Then, finally, she sat down and chose a tea.

"Well, kiddo, what do we do now?" she asked him, and his lips immediately curled into a smile. He supposed he'd never tire of his grandmother calling him kiddo.

"I'm torn," he admitted as he tore off the paper covering the tea bag. "I'm mad. I'm hurt. I'm devastated." He put the tea bag in his mug, sat back, and crossed his legs. "And that's just from my childhood. Fast forward all these years later, and I'm mad, hurt, and devastated that someone would steal from me, hurt my family, and destroy what my friends and I have built. But we've discussed it. We'll rebuild."

His grandmother nodded as she wrapped her tea bag around her spoon and set it on a napkin. "But what about your mother?"

Oliver let out a long breath. "In some ways, I think that's what I was talking about." He reached across the table for his grandmother's hand. "She's broken and we need to help her rebuild."

"She's very broken."

"But only one time. We have to promise ourselves that if she doesn't want to be fixed, and doesn't want to be family, then we need to continue on without her."

"I agree." His grandmother pulled back her hand. "She'll come home to my house. We'll get your old room ready. We'll help her find a job and get on her feet. I want her in her own place in six months."

Oliver wrapped his tea bag around a spoon and gave it a squeeze, then removed it to the napkin his grandmother had used. "Do you think she'll make it?"

His grandmother shrugged. "All we can do is have faith, right?"

"Right," Oliver agreed as he lifted his mug to his lips.

"Okay, that's settled. Now, what about you?"

"What about me?"

His grandmother took two cookies from the jar and handed him one. "What are your plans?"

"Well, once the property is released back to us, we'll start clean up. Paige's brother is a contractor who happens to have time on his hands, and we're going to ask for his help." A smile tugged at his mouth. "Paige suggested that while we rebuild, we run our business out of a tent."

"That's not a shabby idea. A beer garden of sorts," she said thoughtfully.

"I suppose so. I have to run it by the guys, but it has legs."

"And what are you going to do about you and Paige?"

Oliver sipped his tea. "What about me and Paige?"

"When are you going to ask her to marry you?"

Oliver carefully set his mug on the table and puckered his lips. "Grandma, I..."

"Don't tell me you don't know, or some bullshit about it's too soon." When she cursed it always made him laugh, but she was serious and continued. "You're thirty-one years old. You've got a good brain in your head, and a good heart. Some crap got in your way and you're going to make the best of it."

"I am. We are," he agreed.

"So, when are you going to ask her?"

"I'll have to give it some thought. We only discussed it one time, and..."

His grandmother stood, cutting off his thought. She disappeared down the hall to her bedroom and came back a few minutes later with a small box.

She handed it to Oliver, and when he opened it, his eyes welled with tears.

"This is your wedding ring," he said looking up at her standing over him.

"Damn straight it is. Symbol of the strongest marriage I'd ever known. Your grandfather had it made for me. Spent every dime he had and pawned a few other things too so I could have the best. You've found the right girl, Oliver. I think you know that."

He had, there was no doubt about that.

"Give her the ring," his grandmother said. "Plan a wedding for whenever you want down the line. You have a lot going on right now, but commit to her now."

Oliver bit down on his lip and studied the stunning ruby that sparkled up at him. It would look magnificent on Paige's finger.

CHAPTER 46

While Max worked on Paige's studio, Paige helped her sister right her store. There had been some broken glass from the explosion at the tap house, which they'd cleaned up over the weekend. Now items needed to be cleaned off and the store deep cleaned.

Kennedy had cancelled her appointments for the week and wanted to have everything done by Thanksgiving so that the family could be together.

Paige had spoken to her father that morning and he and Gloria had made arrangements to fly in for Thanksgiving and then would leave Friday to spend the weekend with her family.

It was out of his norm, Paige thought, but then again, so had been taking a cruise on a whim and meeting a woman he'd later marry. Life was full of surprises.

Meghann had asked to host Thanksgiving dinner, and Paige thought that by doing that it made her brother finish the remodel on the kitchen faster.

"Are you bringing Oliver to Thanksgiving?" Kennedy asked as she put the purses back on display after having wiped them and the glass they sat on.

"I was going to, but now that you've asked, we didn't discuss it. In fact, I would assume his grandmother would do a Thanksgiving and with his mother getting out of the hospital tomorrow, perhaps they'll want to do their own thing."

Kennedy laughed. "Yep, you're in it fully."

"What does that mean?"

"It means you're truly a couple when you have to contemplate both sides of the family just to have one meal."

"It could be exhausting," Paige admitted as she finished shining the last of the custom jewelry pieces. "What about your mom? Is she planning on you and Max for dinner?"

Kennedy nodded. "Brunch, actually. Meghann thought she could have everything staged before we go to Mom's."

"It's funny when you think of it. Two years ago, Thanksgiving would have been you, Max, your mom and your step-dad. Now it's spouses and a kid."

"Kids," Kennedy said smiling with a shrug.

"Kids?"

"We just found out, so we're not telling anyone yet."

"You're having another baby?" Paige blinked to make sure she had understood.

"Yes. It's the perfect time. Matilda and the baby will be close in age. That was a highlight growing up and having siblings the same age."

Now Paige felt the smile she'd donned retract. "I'll bet that was nice."

Kennedy put down the purse she had in her hand and moved to her sister. "It was something special to have a sister that was little too."

"But I didn't get to go to school with you all or do those kinds of things."

"No, but you had siblings that could drive. And how many sister nights did we have when you were in junior high? How many people can say that?"

Paige laughed. "I miss my mom, but I was always happy to have my big sister."

Kennedy hugged her. "Besides, do you really think you missed out on anything by not having gone to school with Chase? You think he's a trouble maker as an adult? You should have seen him at twelve."

Paige thought about it. Chase was her world when he was twelve and she was three. Perhaps it was because he had a devilish side. Max had always been serious his whole life, and Kennedy had been the coordinator. Not much had changed— except now Paige was having to contemplate multiple Thanksgivings.

"I guess I'll have to see what Oliver's plans are. We plan on meeting at Meghann and Max's at four?" she asked.

Kennedy moved back to the purses. "That's the plan."

Paige went back to cleaning off the jewelry when she looked back up at her sister. "Hey, Ken, congratulations. I'm really happy for you."

WHEN KENNEDY'S store was righted and Paige had stopped by her studio to praise her brother on the progress, she headed home. She wasn't sure where she and Oliver stood on seeing each other daily or even staying with one another. Between the rebuild of the tap house, his mother now in his life and coming home from the hospital, and his grandmother taking care of her, Paige knew his plate was full. It would break her heart if they became distant through it all, but she'd understand.

As she walked through the front door of her house, she dropped her bag to the floor, and walked to the kitchen for a glass of water. Her phone buzzed in her pocket and she took it out to read the text.

Blane needs some company. Would you mind going by my house and checking on him?

He still needed her. Maybe he would need her though the entire process.

I'll head over now, she replied.

Thank you. Key is under the mat.

Seriously?

Paige took a glass down and filled it with water before walking to her bedroom to change out of the clothes she had on. Within the next half hour she was changed, her hair wrapped up in a bun on the top of her, and she was in her car headed to Oliver's.

The house was dark except for the one lamp in his living room, which she knew came on with a timer. Paige parked her car and climbed out, surveying the neighbors just to make sure no one was lurking and would be thinking she was breaking in.

She walked up the front step, pulled back the welcome mat, and sure enough, there was the key. For a guy who had just gone through what he had with someone stealing everything from him, she thought he should be a little more cautious.

Paige slipped the key in the lock and opened the door. To her right was the light switch for the entry, and she turned it on so she could see.

Blane's bell on his collar rang as he pranced from the back of the house to find her.

"Hey, friend. I was told you needed some company."

Paige knelt to pet the cat that brushed up against her legs and noticed that there was a piece of paper tucked under his collar.

"What is this?"

My favorite kitty bowl is in the cupboard.

Paige laughed. "Have you had this on you all day? Your owner is crazy," she teased as she shrugged out of her coat and laid it over one of the chairs in the living room.

Flicking on the light in the kitchen, Paige noticed the vase of roses on the table. Maybe Oliver had brought those home from the hospital after someone had sent them to his mother.

She opened the first cupboard door to find only bags of grains and pastas. Then she opened another and found the plates, cups, and one bowl that was blinged out with Blane's name on it.

She turned to see the cat sitting by the doorway looking toward the laundry room. He was spoiled, she thought.

Paige lifted the bowl and noticed that there was something inside of it. When she lowered it, she realized it was a ring box.

She set the bowl on the counter and picked up the box. Opening it, she saw the most beautiful vintage setting with a large ruby center stone. A smile twitched at the corners of her mouth, and Blane meowed.

When she turned to see what the cat was doing, she watched as Blane moved so that Oliver could walk into the room. He was dressed in a suit, which she hadn't seen him in since her sister had gotten married and he'd stood with Joel.

His hair was perfect and his beard groomed and combed. He was absolutely stunning.

"Your cat seems to have collected some nice things in his food bowl," she said and heard the tears wavering in her voice.

He moved to her taking a rose from the vase. "These are for you. Thanks for coming to feed my cat."

Paige laughed again. "I haven't gotten that far yet," she said taking the rose.

Oliver bent to kiss her gently on the lips.

He took the ring box from her hand and looked at it. "My grandfather had this made for my grandmother. As she put it, he spent everything he had and pawned a few other things just to make sure she had the nicest ring."

"It's beautiful."

"The other night when I was with her, she told me that we were good together. She thought we needed to get married."

"Oh," Paige said, unsure what else she was supposed to say. "She thought that would be a good idea?"

"She does think it's a good idea. And you know what? I happen to agree with her."

"You do?"

Oliver nodded and lowered to one knee.

Paige lifted her hands to cover her mouth as he watched him do so.

"Paige Devereaux, my grandmother is much smarter than I am. She loved a man until he died, and she gave her marriage her all. She raised me to see the value in a good marriage. And now, with you, I think I could have a marriage like my grandparents did. Like your mother and father did."

Oliver took the ring from the box, and set the box on the floor. Then he reached for her hand. "Would you marry me?"

Her lips trembled. Her stomach tightened, and she pressed her hand to it to calm it. "Wow," she said. "I didn't expect this."

"It's the element of surprise."

"I'm surprised."

"But are you in love with me?"

"I am."

"And would you like to live out your days with me?"

"I would."

"So, Paige, will you marry me?"

"I will."

CHAPTER 47

Paige laid in Oliver's arms, the moonlight cascading through the window, and the bell on Blane's collar ringing as he walked through the house.

She twisted the ruby on her finger and smiled. He'd asked her to marry him, and she'd said she would. Chuckling silently, she contemplated the strange week they'd all had, and how it had ended with her in his arms, and a ring on her finger. What would everyone think of that?

"What's on your mind?" Oliver whispered.

"Everything," she said laughing quietly. "This was a disaster of a week—of a month. And yet here we are."

He kissed the top of her head. "One thing I've learned in my life, there's always uncertainty and bad luck. It also seems to follow me," he chuckled. "But then the sun always shines. My grandparents were my sun. My friends were my sun. Our business, this house, and you. Even before I knew I loved you, you were sunshine in my life."

Paige let out a steady breath, hoping to ward off sappy tears. "I don't think you're such bad luck."

"Oh, not me. It just follows me."

She rolled, placing her hand on his chest, and her chin on her hands, she looked up at him. "I guess this is the year of building, right? Max is remodeling his house, my studio, and is going to help you all with the tap room. My dad has a new wife. And between you and me, my sister told me she was pregnant again."

"That's exciting."

"It is."

"Then that can be our theme. New beginnings for the year to come." He brushed his hand over her hair. "My grandmother is going to ask if I followed through with this."

"When should we tell everyone?"

"She wants to have us over for Thanksgiving. I know your family is planning dinner too."

"Kennedy and I were discussing that. Do you think your grandma and mom would want to come to my family's dinner?"

He let out a hum. "Maybe next year. For this year, I think we should keep Mom low key. After all, she's caused a lot of harm to everyone. Or at least in association."

"Meghann is planning for a dinner. Maybe we could plan lunch? Or dinner the night before? I would help cook. I could host even."

Oliver rolled them so that Paige was on her back and he hovered over her. "I'm sure my grandmother will want to host, but we can go together in the morning and talk to her."

"I think we should wait and tell everyone at Thanksgiving. I never get to have big news."

"I think that's a fantastic idea."

He leaned down and kissed her, and that was the end of their conversation.

~

OLIVER HAD NEVER SEEN his grandmother cry, except at his grandfather's funeral. But when he'd taken Paige to see her, and they announced their engagement, she'd cried.

"I knew he needed to marry you. I just knew it," she had said as she kissed Paige's cheeks.

"Thank you for the ring."

"It was good luck for me. Oliver is a lot like his grandfather, and you're a strong and independent woman, so I think it'll be good luck for you too."

They finalized their plans for Thanksgiving dinner on Wednesday night, that way, no one had to run out and they could be a family. And of course, that included Oliver's mother.

Paige had gone to the studio to help Max, and Oliver headed to the hospital to take his mother home.

She was on her way to healing the broken ribs and cuts and bruises, but he wondered if she could now heal herself. After years of being part of a follower to a mission with no cause, and then Mason, she would have to trust that she could be on her own. It had taken a lot of self-talk on Oliver's part, but he was willing to forgive and try to mend their relationship.

His mother was seated in the chair in her room when he arrived.

"It looks like you're ready to go."

She looked up at him with wide eyes that were full of fear. "I don't know if I am. My mother wants me to go home with her, to live with her."

"Yes."

"I don't deserve that."

Oliver knelt down in front of his mother and took her hands. "She loves you. She wants to care for you and I think you need some caring right now."

"What about you? Because of me you lost everything, and so did your friends."

"We're resilient. We will rebuild."

His mother bit down on her lip. "You really think it's a good idea?"

"I do, besides, there's a wedding coming up, and I'd like you to be there for it."

She narrowed her eyes. "A wedding? Who's getting married?"

Oliver smiled widely. "Paige and I are going to get married. I proposed to her last night, and she said yes."

"Oh, Ollie." She batted her eyes and tears rolled down her cheeks. "She's a lovely girl. Oh, my baby is getting married."

Oliver carefully pulled his mother to him and kissed her cheek. Yes, he was willing to start over.

CHAPTER 48

Climbing from Oliver's car, Paige grabbed the pie she had made from the back seat. Oliver came around to take the casserole dish of sweet potatoes he'd made.

The front door was still open, signaling that someone else had just walked inside. As soon as Paige headed up the walk, she could hear the noise that came from inside.

This would be the largest Thanksgiving dinner she'd ever been part of, she decided, and wasn't that invigorating? No longer was it parents and siblings. Now there were spouses and children, and fiancés.

The living room was full of men watching a football game, and Meghann came toward the door to take the items Paige held in her hand to the kitchen.

"Max did a nice job in here," Paige admired.

"He did," Meghann agreed. "I love it. It's completely different than the kitchen I grew up in, and that's good."

Paige kissed her father who was seated at the table with his new wife having a glass of wine. Everything about the day seemed perfect.

Hand in hand, Paige and Oliver walked to the living room

229

where Chase, Max, and Joel sat huddled on the couch watching the game. Paige was sure not one of them saw them walk in. A moment later they all erupted as the football missed the uprights.

As they each picked up their beer to take a drink to drown their sorrows, they looked up at her.

Max stood, kissed her on the cheek. "Hey, sis. What did you think of my kitchen?"

"It's beautiful. You did a good job."

As he passed, Chase stood and shook Oliver's hand, and also kissed Paige on the cheek. "Did you bring that pie you make?"

"It's in the kitchen."

"I'm going to make Meg put a slice on a place for me and keep it safe. Two years, and I haven't gotten a slice. That just isn't fair."

Joel stood from the couch and watched as the team on TV walked to their locker rooms.

"I'm glad I'm not a betting man. I'd have lost," he joked as he moved to shake Oliver's hand. "It's nice to have you here."

"Thanks."

"I have something in the car I need to bring in. Will you help me?" he asked Oliver, and handed Paige his beer as he led Oliver out the door.

OLIVER FOLLOWED Joel to his car, and as they reached it, Joel turned.

"I just wanted to get you out of there for a moment," Joel admitted as he tucked his hands into the front pockets of his jeans. "First of all, I want to say I'm sorry for everything."

"Joel—"

"No, let me finish. You're a brother to me, and at the first sign of trouble, I told you to stay home. I always knew in my heart you did nothing wrong. It's not in your makeup."

"Thanks."

"And I know the others have the same to tell you. We all feel awful."

"You're right. We're all brothers. I know you all have my back."

Joel nodded. "We do. That's what I wanted to talk to you about. Kennedy and I are here for you if you need anything. And I mean anything at all. I know that finances for you are going to suck for a while. That S.O.B. took everything from you."

"Not everything."

"Financially," Joel chuckled. "We have a nice nest egg and we'd like to share it with you."

Oliver shook his head. "That is mighty generous, and I'll let you know if I need anything."

"Promise?"

"I promise."

THE DINING ROOM table had been extended and two more card tables had been set at the end of the dining table and it extended into the kitchen. Paige thought it was the most magnificent sight ever.

It had been Gloria that said prayer, and Paige was grateful. For some reason, just the thought of being the one to say grace at the meal gave her anxiety.

As Gloria ended the prayer, she lifted her glass of wine. "I would like to thank you all for having us here this year. I am honored to be part of this amazing family."

They each lifted their glasses in return, and Paige thought it was the perfect time to give their announcement.

As she took a breath to speak, Kennedy tapped her glass. "Joel, Matilda, and I have an announcement too," she said as her cheeks pinked. "We're having another baby."

As expected, the room grew loud with excitement before

Chase stood from his seat. "Good news and good fortune is abundant, I guess. Hillary and I were waiting until today to share that we are having another baby, too. We applied for adoption, and just yesterday were told that we have a baby. She'll be here in a few months."

Now the room grew louder as laughter roared and congratulations were passed along. When Max pulled Meghann to her feet, Chase leaned back in his chair. "Are you kidding me?"

Max wrapped his arm around Meghann's shoulders. "What kind of sibling rivalry would this be if we didn't try to one up you?"

Kennedy's brow rose. "How do you one up that?"

"Twins!" Meghann nearly burst.

Now Paige's siblings were all out of their chairs and embracing one another. Oliver held her hand under the table and gave it a squeeze. He must have felt her tense. What good was her announcement now?

As everyone settled back into their seats and began to pass the dishes of food around, Paige kept her eyes averted from everyone. She was afraid she just might cry, and it wasn't worth it. They would all celebrate her news and she knew it.

"Paige, will you pass me the potatoes?" Kennedy asked.

Paige picked up the bowl and held it across the table for her sister to take. Kennedy took the bowl with one hand and quickly grabbed Paige's hand with the other.

"This is new," Kennedy admired the ruby on Paige's finger.

Now the tears did roll down her cheeks.

"Paige, what's wrong?"

Oliver stood and pulled Paige to her feet, wrapping his arm around her shoulders. "I think Paige and I can agree that the past few months have been a roller coaster of emotions, endings, and new beginnings. Today, I think that proves that point more than any. Four new babies to join this amazing family, which I've been lucky enough to be included in since Joel and Kennedy met."

Paige wiped the tears from her cheek and looked up at Oliver, who kissed her forehead.

"I think Paige would like to make an announcement too," Oliver continued.

Paige let out a slow and controlled breath and looked at Kennedy. "The ring is his grandmother's. She gave it to him and told him he should marry me."

The room was silent, and all eyes were locked on Paige.

Kennedy looked around. "And? Did he ask you to marry him?"

"Yes, and I said yes."

Kennedy was the first from her seat and she rounded the long table to get to the other side and wrap Paige in her arms. "Oh, my God! My baby sister is getting married."

Hillary and Meghann pulled her in, and before she knew it, everyone was out of their seats.

When her father moved to her and took her face in his hands, he pressed a kiss to her forehead. "Be happy, Paige. Be very happy."

EPILOGUE

Work on the tap room had continued as beer was served from a large tent in the parking lot. By July, everything was back to normal, and just in time to celebrate the fourth in style.

Paige's studio had grown to include yoga, tai chi, massage, and she had hired an acupuncturist, which - just the word - made her sister queasy.

When Oliver's mother was physically healthy, and had the blessing of her therapist, she had decided she'd wanted to move out on her own. Oliver knew that the best place for her was in his house, and by summer, he'd moved in with Paige and they'd begun to make their home. They'd planted a new tree and a fresh garden to signify the new beginning they were starting.

They had decided on a Thanksgiving wedding, because it had seemed like the right time. They certainly were grateful for the year that had come and eased the pain of the year before.

And, just like her sister, Paige and Oliver thought the tap house was the perfect place to have their wedding surrounded by those that they loved.

As Paige studied herself in the mirror of her sister's store, she smiled at the simple, white, cotton dress and the halo of daisies in her hair.

Hillary spritzed Paige's hair with hair spray once more. "You're stunning. Just stunning."

"I feel like I'm playing dress up," Paige admitted.

Kennedy moved in behind her and placed a necklace on her neck. "Dad wanted you to have this. It was your mom's."

Paige bit down on her lip as it began to tremble and she reached her hand to the locket that Kennedy had clasped on her. When she opened it, there was a picture of her as a baby on one side, and a photo of her parents on the other.

"This is one of the most precious things I've ever been given."

Kennedy nodded as she wiped the tear from her eye, careful not to mess up her makeup.

"Are you ready?" her father's voice came from behind her.

"More than ever," Paige said as she moved to him and kissed his cheek. "Thank you for the necklace."

"She wanted you to have it on your wedding day. I've made Kennedy hold on to it. She's had it for years."

And that made Paige's chest swell.

"I'm ready."

OLIVER STOOD in the tap house surrounded by their family and friends. They had decided on a circle of chairs so they would be surrounded by everyone they loved. As he looked around, he realized just how much had changed in the past three years since they'd purchased the building and began planning the tap house.

Joel held his new daughter on his shoulder, and Kennedy bounced their toddler Matilda on her knee.

Hillary cradled her son in her arms, and Gloria had soft conversations with little Kennedy who sat on her knee and touched her grandmother's jewelry.

Max had his son on his shoulder and Meghann held their daughter in the crook of her arm.

Oliver's mother sat next to his grandmother. She looked healthy and happy, and he was so glad to have her there. It would take a lot of work to move past the twenty-three years they'd been apart, but they were working on it.

When the door to the tap house opened, he saw Paige for the first time that day, on the arm of her father.

It was all he could do to stand still with the minister and wait for her to walk to him.

When they arrived in the center of the room, her father kissed her cheek and shook Oliver's hand.

"You look beautiful," he said as Paige's smile widened.

"And you, you're so handsome."

He took her hand and pressed a kiss to it. "This is just the start of an amazing adventure."

"I can't wait to take it with you."

"I love you, Paige Devereaux."

"Oliver Westcott, I love you, too," she said before they both turned to the minister who went through all of the things to make them officially married, but inside he knew his soul had always belonged to Paige, and would forever.

ABOUT THE AUTHOR

Bestselling Author Bernadette Marie is known for building families readers want to be part of. Her series The Keller Family has graced bestseller charts since its release in 2011. Since then she has authored and published over forty books. The married mother of five sons promises romances with a *Happily Ever After always*...and says she can write it because she lives it.

Obsessed with the art of writing and the business of publishing, chronic entrepreneur Bernadette Marie established her own publishing house, 5 Prince Publishing, in 2011 to bring her own work to market as well as offer an opportunity for fresh voices in fiction to find a home as well. Bernadette is also an educator in the industry, offering workshops and speaking at conferences. In 2020 she was named the Independent Writer of the Year from the Rocky Mountain Fiction Writers.

When not immersed in the writing/publishing world, Bernadette Marie and her husband are watching their five hockey playing boys as well as running their family business. Bernadette is an avid Martial Artist with a second degree black belt in Tang Too Do, is a lover of a good stout craft beer, and might be slightly addicted to chocolate.

OTHER TITLES FROM

5 PRINCE PUBLISHING

www.5princebooks.com

Paige Devereaux *Bernadette Marie*
Max Devereaux *Bernadette Marie*
Christmas Cookies on a Cruise Ship *Parker Fairchild*
Chase Devereaux *Bernadette Marie*
Kennedy Devereaux *Bernadette Marie*
The Seven Spires *Russell Archey*
At Last *Bernadette Marie*
Masterpiece *Bernadette Marie*
A Tropical Christmas *Bernadette Marie*
Corporate Christmas *Bernadette Marie*
Faith Through Falling Snow *Sandy Sinnett*
Walker Defense *Bernadette Marie*
Clash of the Cheerleaders *April Marcom*
Stevie-Girl and the Phantom of Forever *Ann Swann*
Assemble the Party *Antony Soehner*
The Last Goodbye *Bernadette Marie*
The Gingerbread Curse *April Marcom*
Stevie-Girl and the Phantom of Crybaby Bridge *Ann Swann*

241

The MacBrides: Hannah & Ash *J.L. Petersen*
Leather and Lies *Celeste Straub*
Beginnings *Bernadette Marie*
Love and Loopholes *Railyn Stone*
Unite The Party *Antony Soehner*
Star Seer *April Marcom*
Totally Devoted *E.M. Bannock*
Bases Loaded *Jena James*
The Tea Shop *Bernadette Marie*

PLEASE REVEIW

We hope you enjoyed Paige Devereaux by Bernadette Marie. If you did, we would ask that you please rate and review this title. Every review helps our authors.

Rate and Review: Paige Devereaux

5 Prince Publishing
Arvada, Colorado, USA